Daughters
of *the*
House

MICHÈLE ROBERTS

OTHER WORKS BY MICHÈLE ROBERTS

FICTION
A Piece of the Night
The Visitation
The Wild Girl
The Book of Mrs Noah
In the Red Kitchen

POETRY
The Mirror of the Mother
Psyche and the Hurricane

FILM
The Heavenly Twins

PLAYS
The Journeywoman

She has also co-authored four books of poetry
and four collections of short stories

Published by VIRAGO PRESS Limited 1992
20–23 Mandela Street, Camden Town, London NW1 0HQ

Copyright © Michèle Roberts

The right of Michèle Roberts to be identified as the author of
this work has been asserted by her in accordance with the
Copyright, Designs and Patents Act 1988

A CIP catalogue record for this book
is available from the British Library

Typeset by Falcon Typographic Art Ltd, Fife, Scotland
Printed in Great Britain

Author's Note

A major source of inspiration for this novel was *L'histoire d'une âme* by Thérèse Martin, who is more often known as Saint Thérèse of the Child Jesus, also as The Little Flower. Just as my Thérèse is a fictional character, so the village of Blémont-la-Fontaine is an imaginary one, its inhabitants existing only on paper.

My thanks to Caroline Dawnay, Lennie Goodings, Jim Latter and Elsbeth Lindner for reading and criticizing earlier drafts of this novel.

for Beewee

THE WALL

*I*t was a changeable house. Sometimes it felt safe as a church, and sometimes it shivered, then cracked apart.

A sloping blue slate roof held it down. Turrets at the four corners wore pointed blue hats. The many eyes of the house were blinded by white shutters.

What bounded the house was skin. A wall of gristle a soldier could tear open with his bare hands. Antoinette laughed. She was buried in the cellar under a heap of sand. Her mouth was stuffed full of torn-up letters and broken glass but she was tunnelling her way out like a mole. Her mouth bled from the corners. She laughed a guttural laugh, a Nazi laugh.

The house was strict. The rules indicated the forbidden places. Chief of these was the bedroom at the back on the first floor, at the top of the kitchen stairs. (second floor in N. Am.)

The rules said you mustn't go there. It was for your own protection. Each time Léonie tried, she had to halt. The terror was so strong. It pushed her away, wouldn't let her come near. Behind the terror was something evil which stank and snarled and wanted to fix her in its embrace. Better to flee, to clatter back across the bare plank floor of the landing, find the headlong stairs and fall down them. Better to stay at the front of the house.

Antoinette was dead, which was why they had buried her in the cellar. She moved under the heap of sand. She clutched her red handbag, which was full of shreds of dead flesh. She was trying to get out, to hang two red petticoats on the washing-line in the orchard. Sooner or later she would batter down the cellar door and burst up through it on her dead and bleeding feet.

The deadness and the evil and the stink were inside Léonie. She rushed up the cellar steps, magically she erupted into her own bed in the dark, the smell of warm blood, soaked sawdust.

Now she was properly awake. She ran to the bathroom to be sick. It was Thérèse she was throwing up. She vomited her forth, desperate to be rid of her and then weak with gasping relief that she was gone.

THE WRITING-TABLE

*L*éonie was waiting for Thérèse to arrive. She longed for her, like a lover. Her mind bristled with knives. She imagined the edge of the blade, silvery and saw-toothed. Its tip vanishing into Thérèse's soft flesh.

She could not settle. She paced up and down the corridor in which things had stood in their places since long before she was born. The little buttoned armchair in worn pink brocade. The two porcelain jars, plump dragons, that guarded the writing-table. The mirror with its broken-pediment frame. The strip of silk carpet, bald in places, frayed.

These items her eyes checked one by one. They were hers. As the house was. Hers to dispose of as she wished and thought proper. She would not share them with Thérèse. She had cared for the house, spent her money on it, kept it in good repair. All these years of tending it meant that it was hers.

This morning she had begun listing the house contents in the inventory her lawyer had suggested she draw up. But she was too excited to go on. She would continue with her task once Thérèse had arrived and settled in. She wondered how long she ought to wait before asking Thérèse about her plans. She promised herself to be very tactful, very discreet.

The writing-table stood against the wall, facing it, halfway down the corridor which ran, on the first floor, along the back of the house. Antoinette, in the days when she was well enough, had sat here to write notes of invitation, letters to her sisters. Madeleine, and then Léonie, had gone on using her pen, blue ink, leather-bound blotter. Léonie perched here, on the curvy-backed chair with a tapestry seat, to do her accounts. And now the inventory.

The mirror opposite her flickered a warning. Which of us is which? For twenty years she had cohabited peacefully with her reflection, peering at it to check that she'd got what she thought she'd got. Yes, she existed, the mirror told her over those years: with her smooth surface, fresh gilding, only a little tarnish. Now that other one was turning up, to disrupt her steady gaze.

When she looked at Thérèse, what would she see? She supposed they had both aged. If she smashed her fist into Thérèse's face, would she hear the crack and splinter of glass? She wondered whether Thérèse's sheltered life had kept her looking young. When they were both sixteen she had been pleased to make comparisons. She had better legs than Thérèse, a sharper clothes sense, a more fashionably slender body. When Thérèse arrived she would be able to carry on that old war.

Up and down she paced. She liked the sound of her footsteps measuring the long silence of the corridor. As she liked the fact that the corridor had doors at both ends, represented both pause and process. Was not a room but was between rooms. Both connected and separated them.

When you came up the curve of the oval staircase on to the first floor, you arrived in a hallway set with doors half-concealed in grey panelling. Opening the furthest on the left, you passed into a second, tiny, hall, off which opened Antoinette's old bedroom and the bathroom. A third grey-painted door, part of the panelling like all the others, led out of this little lobby into the corridor.

Thérèse would remember which door was which. She would not arrive, as Léonie still did in her dreams, as a stranger, confused by the labyrinth that was the house, discovering the corridor at the back as a surprise. Thérèse would walk into the house as her birthright, the place she'd lived in all through her childhood. She would see Léonie as the usurper, Léonie as the one who stole what was not hers to inherit. Thérèse the prodigal would return wanting everything.

Would Thérèse remember the room at the other end of the corridor, and what it had once held? Did she ever dream of trying to walk into it in the dark? Did she ever wake, in a thrash of sweat, trembling and clenched, in her bed that for twenty years had been safely foreign and far away?

Léonie found that she was downstairs, in the centre of the kitchen. A rack of knives hung on the wall near the hood of the fireplace. Symmetry of thick black handles implanted with thin blades, razor fine. In English, she remembered explaining to Thérèse once: *wicked* could mean *sharp*. There was a gap in the row of knives. Léonie looked down, puzzled, at her hands. She discovered she was testing the tip of the vegetable knife, the ancient one with the ragged edge, against her thumb. She raised it. She divided the air in two. Then she let the knife drop on to the kitchen table.

She felt dizzy. As though Thérèse were already here and they were children again, playing that game of spinning on one spot with arms outstretched, seeing who could twirl longest and not fall.

THE DOORBELL

*T*hérèse arrived by bus. She insisted that she did not want to
be met. I'm quite capable of walking, she told Léonie over
the phone: I've still got the use of my legs, you know, and my brain,
I haven't forgotten the way.

No scenes in public, was what she meant. Not that she expected
Léonie to fall on her neck and call for the fatted calf to be slain. But she
felt raw, as though she'd been flayed, all her old customs and gestures
stripped off along with the brown dress she'd worn for twenty years.
She didn't want to stand out, or be recognized. She would slink into
the village anonymous and discreet. She would cover her face until
she was ready to show it. She asked Léonie not to tell people she
was coming back. No fuss. Let them find out in the ordinary course
of things. To herself she added: when I've decided exactly what it is
I must do.

The bus plunged along the banks of the Seine. Thérèse remembered
strings of ancient houses, black and cream displays of timbering,
plaster, thatch. The great flat river sliding between cliffs. A calm
green emptiness which turned in spring to a pink carnival of flowering
orchards. How many new houses there were now, how very tidy and
rebuilt everything seemed. *Restored*, that was the word one used.
Corrected. Freshened.

She felt peculiar. It was her clothes, she decided. Her knees exposed
by the skirt of her dress riding up when she sat down. Her legs, nude
in fawn nylons. Her general sense of skimpy coverings, of being too
visible. In the bus she was a focus for others' glances, however casual,
and she resented it.

When at Caudebec a couple of Algerian men got on to the bus
Thérèse stared at them. Black people didn't live in the green

Norman countryside. Surely they all lived in ghettoes on the outskirts of cities.

Mutters from the other passengers reached her.

A bad lot, I'm afraid, always looking for trouble.

Far too many of them coming in.

Thérèse turned her head aside and gazed out of the window. Billboards hoisted posters in Gothic lettering that advertised ancient inns, traditional cider and Calvados, authentic butter and cheese. Grandmother's this and that, everything from pine furniture to apricot jam. The signs all pointed somewhere else: over there; that's the real thing. Then the bus jolted around a sharp corner with a blare of its horn and they swept into Blémont's little main street.

The bus-stop, just as in the old days, was the area of pavement outside the *Mairie*. This florid building was now painted salmon pink, no longer the faded grey that Thérèse remembered. She shrugged, watching the bus depart, backside of blue glass farting exhaust. She stooped to pick up her bags.

At the top of the street behind her was the village church. Beyond it, the cemetery, and the family grave. Her mother was buried there under a slab of polished granite, and her father, and his second wife Madeleine. In a far corner, separated from the fields beyond by a high wall, was the grave of Henri Taillé. His bones had been found eventually and brought here, and the tangle of bones of the unknown Jews buried with him. The shallow pit had opened and given them up. She wondered whether she should go there now, to see for herself what she had read about in the newspaper. The grave newly opened and desecrated, swastikas in red daubed on the tombstone. The church bells tolling gently decided her. She didn't want to be seen by the people turning out for early-evening Mass. She'd visit the cemetery in the morning. She would go very early, before anyone was about, and check the evidence with her own eyes.

She crossed the road, to take the turning that led off between the chemist's and the blacksmith's. Oh. There was no longer a blacksmith's. And the chemist's window, which used to contain antique apothecary pots in *vieux Rouen* porcelain, was now full of strip-lit placards of naked women scrubbing their thighs with green mittens. What was cellulite? Thérèse walked on.

She told herself that she was calm. That she was on the right road. That her feet did recognize its bends and loops. There was a pavement now, streetlamps and bus-shelters on this stretch, signs warning of sharp corners, an old people's home. The old school had been knocked down and a new one, prefab style, built in its place, next to an asphalt playground. Only half a kilometre on did the countryside as she remembered it burst upon her. She smelled grass, wet earth, manure. She saw tall poplars and beech trees flicker like feathers as the wind stirred them. She recognized the profiles of familiar barns.

The tall white wrought-iron gates stood open. Beyond them the little white manor-house floated in its courtyard of white gravel. The long lawn at one side was still surrounded by beds of silvery and white flowers. The massive cedar at its far end still looked like part of a stage-set. Thérèse gripped her bags more firmly and went forward.

Even though it was late afternoon there were no lights on in the house. Everything was still. As though Léonie had gone away. The windows did not blaze yellow as Thérèse wanted them to, did not burn, flags of welcome to herself, weary traveller, sister returning from exile. She trod across the gravel and pressed the white enamel doorbell under the little wrought-iron and glass porch. Light came on behind the long glass panels of the door. Someone wrenched it open from inside. It scraped and squeaked on the tiled floor of the hall, just as it always had. A woman with angry eyes under a shining fringe peered out. It was Léonie.

THE CHANDELIER

The chandelier was made of metal twisted into leaves painted pale green. These twined about sprays of flowers, red stars with yellow hearts. Nestling in this hard wreath were improbable fruits, lemon-coloured globes of glass. The chandelier hung from one of the white iron struts that crisscrossed, in arches, the roof of the little conservatory at the back of the house. Thérèse, coming into it, was reminded of the railway station where she had broken her journey earlier that day: the draughty cold, the glass-and-metal-domed roof, the shadowy corners. Then Léonie, beside her, put out a hand and depressed a switch and the circlet of glass lemons dangling above their heads sprang into vibrant colour, gleamed out in yellow.

Chill struck up into Thérèse's feet from the grey tiles, speckled with red, that she stood on. Cold prickled inside her nose, around her neck and wrists. She tucked her hands into the sleeves of her cardigan, regretting having let Léonie take her coat. Why did Léonie choose to sit here of all places? Shivering, she looked about. The old wicker armchairs, their red and black paint almost completely worn off, still surrounded the wicker table. Scarlet and pink geraniums were rampant on all sides, just as they used to be. She snuffed up their rough fragrance. What was new was the plethora of vases, standing on every available surface, stuffed with sheaves of wheat, oats and barley. Someone had been busy transforming some of these into corn plaits and twists, which hung from the shelves supporting the geranium pots. The straw stalks were pale and glossy, woven into their ridged patterns by an obviously expert hand. Had Léonie taken up making corn dollies?

Light from the chandelier fell on Léonie's fair hair, two walls of satin that dropped exactly to jaw level. She wore black linen trousers, a brown silk polo-neck, expensively narrow shoes. Léonie was nearly forty, her blue eyes nested in crow's-feet and wrinkles, and she was a lot plumper than formerly. But there was something childish about her that made her seem younger than she was. Good skin, thought Thérèse: good legs. Why does that matter so much?

It always had. The right body, right clothes, right way of talking, of attracting and pleasing others: Thérèse hadn't had it. No, she thought: something much deeper, inside, that I felt I lacked, I didn't know what it was. Femininity? Not a real woman like the others? Had Léonie ever felt that?

She felt Léonie's eyes scamper over her. Now she would have to compete. She couldn't bear Léonie to see her in these ugly clothes she'd been given to come home in. Pale blue synthetic-stuff dress with ill-matching blue cardigan, navy court shoes that pinched. She wrapped her arms around herself and glared at a corn wreath twined with gold ribbon.

Oh those, Léonie chattered with a wave of her hand: leftover decorations for the harvest festival. It's tomorrow. I told you the date in my letter, remember? You'll see tomorrow, in church, the decorations are wonderful. Baptiste thinks it's important to keep up the old crafts. He says we mustn't let the old Norman traditions die out. You of all people should agree with that.

Thérèse shrugged, not knowing what to reply. She felt rusty. Not used to sociability. She glanced upwards for inspiration.

I'm glad you've still got the chandelier, she said: I remember when Papa put that up. He brought it back from Italy, he and Maman.

Of course I've still got it, Léonie said: why on earth would I want to get rid of it? Everything in this house that's old, that belonged to our family, is precious to me. I'd never get rid of anything.

So much anger prickled in the air between them that they took a step away from each other. Thérèse's feet fizzed. There was a tremor in her knees.

In a hurry Léonie said: Let's have a drink. We'll have supper later. I'll go and get some ice. Will you fetch the bottle and glasses? You know where they're kept. You know where the *buffet* is.

THE BUFFET

*T*he clock had not changed. Its tick was the heavy heartbeat of the house, slow, the fall of metal brushes. It had measured out Thérèse's childhood. Moment after moment of endless afternoons. She'd forgotten it. Now, after twenty years, she heard it again.

The *buffet* stood in its old place opposite the clock. In one corner of the white-panelled dining-room, between the window, hung with frilled muslin, and the door out into the hall. The door-handle was a china egg, cold in her palm. Loose, it still wobbled, exactly as it used to. The door rattled, just as it had always done.

A local craftsman had made the *buffet* for the wedding of Thérèse's grandparents. It would have been hers if she had married. A solid piece in worn pine, darkened with age, satin-smooth. Its top pair of doors was carved with reliefs of oakleaf garlands. Two fat swags that hung down, one on each door. To open the *buffet* you didn't bother tugging at the key but instead inserted your finger into a silky hole at the base of one of the doors, and pulled.

Inside, on the top shelf, was the old arrangement of bottles of cassis, Bénédictine, Calvados and rum, glass flasks of oil and vinegar, blue pots of salt and mustard. On the middle shelf, just as before, were rows of wine and water glasses, stacks of dessert plates. On the bottom shelf lay neatly folded napkins and tablecloths. The napkin-cases laboriously embroidered by Thérèse and Léonie long ago, wobbly red cross-stitch on blue checked gingham, were still there.

Thérèse could not stop shivering. Thrifty Léonie had denied the cold in the house. It's only September. Far too early in the season to switch on the heating. So Antoinette's early training had held good with this most unlikely of candidates. Deny the body's needs and advance in holiness. Then Thérèse felt ashamed. Probably Léonie *was* hard up, running a house this size and with all those children to bring up. Who am I to criticize? Thérèse thought: for twenty years I haven't earned my own living, for twenty years I've been able to be irresponsible as a child.

She spotted a small woollen blanket padding one of the chairs drawn up to the dining-table. She picked it up, wrapped it about her shoulders. It smelled strongly of cat but she was too cold and tired to care. She took two glasses and a bottle of gin from the *buffet*, put them on the tray she found on a nearby side-table. A wizened lemon lurked in a glass bowl. But no tonic. She would have to go and see whether it was kept in the kitchen. Don't rush, she told herself: it's only your first alcoholic drink in twenty years.

She went the long way round. Deliberately chose to take a detour, so that she could make a quick check on the house and on her memories of it. See whether Léonie had hung hideous examples of craft work all over the place or moved the furniture about. She tiptoed through all the rooms on the ground floor, lighting them one by one as she opened their doors then plunged through them and left them behind her in the dark again. Fragrance of potpourri in some places, of furniture polish, of cats, of dust. More corn dollies. Fussy arrangements of dried flowers. Modern children's litter of tennis rackets, records, board games. Curved tunnel of rooms, one leading out of, into, another. Thérèse forgot her wish to inspect for changes, instead fell into wonder.

Léonie could choose to sit in any one of three *salons*, small medium big, or in the conservatory. More rooms upstairs, on two floors. How dared she have so much choice, so much freedom of movement? Thérèse remembered the bare cell she had left behind her, the half-hour daily allotted to exercise. Dully walking up and down between two brick walls. In this house you could stride.

In the old days she had not noticed its size. It was home, and it was full of people. Her child's eye had not been overwhelmed by these chilly mausoleums Antoinette called sitting-rooms, had created the spaces she needed, her own small ones she could pull round her. Tonight she was unsure of her size as she blundered through the dark. She stumbled on a stone step and fell into the kitchen.

It was just as she remembered it. A large square room dominated by its blackleaded range. Wooden table, carved dresser stacked with bowls and plates. The wall of the chimney breast above the range, and the wall above the marble shelf where the eggs were still kept, she was pleased to see, in a wire basket, were decorated with old blue and white tiles. The kitchen was dark. Blackened. That was how she'd seen it as a child. A cave, in whose shadowy corners swam blue figures on a cream ground, the gleam and streak of marble. Now a modern cooker squeezed in next to the range. A new fridge, bright white, jutted behind the back door. Smart white spotlights wreathed their plastic necks above the table and cooker. Sensible enough, Thérèse supposed, and doubtless Victorine would have approved. At the moment the kitchen was lit by two candles set in flowered china candlesticks in front of the little plaster Virgin on a bracket on the wall. Others of Victorine's household gods remained too. The tin picture of a vase of roses nailed above the fridge. The white linen drying-up cloths, with a single red stripe, hung from the side of the sink. The wooden plate-rack above the draining-board. The shallow wicker basket of red onions that stood next to the eggs on the marble shelf. If she ignored the cooker and the fridge then hardly anything had changed. Too much attachment to objects, she scolded herself. She had spent twenty years trying to practise detachment and she had failed. She'd discovered that as soon as she had re-entered the house.

My house, Thérèse corrected herself softly: *my* house. All of it.

She opened the fridge and took out the bottle of tonic.

THE BED

*T*he tablecloth was thick, smooth and blue. Heavy Indian cotton, a thin turquoise line through blue checks. Small frayed holes here and there. Thérèse remembered pushing bored fingers through those openings, to enlarge them. Lunches in childhood had gone on so long.

Léonie insisted on laying the table properly, even though they were only going to eat in the kitchen. She twitched the cloth so that it hung evenly, flattened its rumples with a brisk hand. No excuse for being sloppy, things need to be done right. Thérèse could hear Victorine's monitoring voice as though she were in the room. Her heart unlocked and let out sayings she didn't know she'd stored.

She sat with her back pressed against the white metal pleats of the radiator. On the sidelines of this busy kitchen life. Wanting just to observe. She fiddled with her glass, sipped from it. Sparkly sweetness of gin and tonic, quinine, on her tongue. She felt twirled about, giddy. Drinking too fast.

Léonie put a rustic brown pottery jug, full of water, on the table. Its glaze was silvery. Zigzags had been cut in the clay before firing. She flanked it with an open bottle of red wine, the two flowered candlesticks from the bracket on the wall. One white candle and one cream-coloured. Their flames danced then steadied, climbing yellow about the sturdy black wicks. Two dark primrose soup plates in thick porcelain with wide fluted edges. Big silver soup spoons, silver forks, black-handled knives. The old cutlery Thérèse remembered. Placed by Léonie just so. A basket of chopped bread. Shining red pot of leek and potato soup with cream poured in. Hunger growled in her like a dog. She pulled up her chair to the table. Léonie sat opposite. In the calm golden glow of the candles they ate.

Soup just like Victorine used to make, Léonie said: of course. I use all her old recipes.

You think you've laid a real French supper, Thérèse thought: but you haven't got it quite right. I know that. But you don't. You grew up in England, don't forget. You with your peasant-style pots and your corn dollies. If she were alive Victorine would laugh at you.

She could only pick at her slice of roast veal in rich gravy.

I'm sorry, she apologized: I'm not used to such good food. Back there we always ate so simply.

She heard herself sounding priggish, felt herself flush. She watched Léonie reach for more *petits pois* and veal.

I'm too greedy I expect, Léonie said: food matters to me too much probably.

She pointed with her fork at Thérèse.

But you're so thin. Just skin and bone. Are you ill?

She doesn't want me to look good, Thérèse thought: slimmer than she is. Easier to see me as a burden, a sick person she'll have to look after, she's worried she'll never get me off her hands.

Eating sensibly, she declared: is crucial for health, a well-balanced diet and not too much of anything that's my motto.

Léonie laughed unwillingly over her heaped plate: Thérèse had imitated Victorine's voice and manner so precisely. But she was obviously angry: her gifts rejected, her control waved aside. Thérèse sat back, pleased with herself. Pleased too with her flat stomach, lean hips. No longer the fat girl she'd been as an adolescent. Her body obeyed her now. She watched Léonie mop her plate with a piece of bread and eat it with relish, pour herself more wine. Léonie used to be skinny as a boy. No one could call her too thin these days, that was certain.

She finally remembered to ask.

How's Baptiste? Where is he tonight? And where are the girls? Have you drowned them all three or what?

Baptiste's got a meeting in the village, Léonie said: you remember, he's the mayor now, I did write and tell you. And the girls, they're scattered all over the place. Summer camp. Staying with friends. Travelling. The house is so quiet, I feel like a ghost in it.

They did kiss each other good night. As they had kissed on meeting. A brushing of cheeks, the lips kept well away from contact with skin. Léonie's obvious excuse being that she had thick red lipstick on. She used to ask Thérèse for kisses: a real

— 15 —

big smacker that's what I want. Pain woke and stretched inside Thérèse.

She said: I'm so tired, I must go to bed, we'll have a proper chat tomorrow won't we.

Of course, Léonie said.

Thérèse picked up the larger of her two bags from where Léonie had dumped them earlier in the hall. She started up the stairs with it. Her body sagged with fatigue.

Don't worry about the other one, Léonie called up after her: I'll bring it up for you later on.

Don't bother, Thérèse said: I don't need it. Not tonight anyway.

Léonie had given Thérèse the best bedroom. The one that the Martin parents used to sleep in together before Antoinette moved to the smaller one next door, nearer the bathroom. Louis had gone on sleeping in this one, alone. Then later on he had moved downstairs. Thérèse wondered a little at Léonie's choice of room to offer her. Tomorrow she would pick at motives, admitted and secret. Tonight she was merely relieved that her fingers knew exactly where to find the round end of the light-switch just inside the door. Where the hand-basin hid behind a faded blue curtain. How to unhook the fastenings of the little white cupboards on either side of the oblong sink.

His things. All these years after his death they were still here. Zipped brown leather case containing silver-backed brushes and silver-topped bottles. White china seashell embracing Roget Gallet tea-rose soap. Folded linen towels for face and hands. The room was a shrine, relics lovingly preserved. Intact. Dusted, washed, ironed. By Léonie? Thérèse's feet slipped her away, over the embroidered cotton rugs, towards the bed.

This stood in the far corner opposite the door, its mattress fitted into a mahogany frame curved and scrolled at top and bottom. Next to it was a little marble-topped stand bearing a lamp, a fluted green glass with a white rose in it. Under the glass was a square white cloth with a lace edge, starched, glossily flat.

Thérèse sank into plumy depths. The mattress was as cushiony as the quilt encased in red silk, the pillow large and square. Bedding luxurious as cream.

The wallpaper was still the same. A design of tiny sprigs of pink and cream roses on what had been once, Thérèse remembered, a brilliant blue background and was faded now to a pleasing indigo. She stared at the crucifix which hung on the wall opposite her, at the slender switch of palm tucked behind the ivory Christ. Her hands went up to check the cotton scarf she had tied around her head.

She'd been born in this bed. She rolled over, she felt she must, to make space for her mother beside her, newly delivered after a day and a night of labour.

THE HOLDALL

*L*éonie waited half an hour, until she was sure Thérèse must be asleep. She balanced outside her bedroom door, breath hushed and ears cocked. No sound. No halo of light between door and frame.

She glided back downstairs. She'd seen Thérèse's look travel scornfully over her plumpness, oh yes, but at least she was still light on her feet. She made a good spy. Now she needed to hurry. Before Baptiste got home. She didn't want him to catch her rifling through Thérèse's things.

She picked up the holdall from where Thérèse had left it at the bottom of the stairs and took it into the kitchen. Pushing aside the debris of supper things she dumped it on the table. She shook her head at it. Ugly and cheap, like the clothes Thérèse had arrived home in. Blue plastic, with a worn strap. She told herself she was justified in looking inside. To keep one step ahead in this uneasy game.

It wasn't locked. So it wasn't private, really. And leaving it around was just asking for someone to open it. She tugged the zip past places where it stuck, wrenched the bag's mouth apart. Words were inside. Books. She lifted them out. Paperbacks mainly. Modern French history. Jewish history. Léonie's fingers came up to pull at her lower lip.

Underneath the volumes of history, at the bottom of the holdall, was a notebook. Pages covered in Thérèse's well-behaved rounded script. She wrote in blue ballpoint, a cheap one that left thick blue blots. Léonie's own name cropped up quite a lot. Stuff about their childhood.

Léonie flicked over the leaves of squared paper, then turned back to the first page. Thérèse had written her title with flourishes, had underlined it three times. *The story of a soul.* Léonie grimaced. Presumably Thérèse was now an expert in such matters.

Léonie went to Mass every Sunday with her husband and children. It was what you did, like going to school, going to the clinic to give birth. What she liked best about Sundays was going to the baker's afterwards to buy cakes for lunch, then coming home to hot chocolate and a slice of *galette*, sipping her *apéritif* while relishing the smell of roast lamb from the kitchen.

Thérèse had listed words like *soul, God, sin, miracle, prayer.* Léonie's inventory sang a litany of beds and tables and chairs. I haven't got a soul, have I, she thought: Thérèse stole it.

THE GREY SILK NIGHTSHIRT

*T*hérèse yawned into her pillow. A silky bag of feathers held in a linen envelope. Too big and fat. There was too much of everything in this house. Too much food, too much drink, too much noise. She had heard Léonie come to her door, stand there listening, go away again. She had heard Baptiste arrive home, car tyres scattering the gravel and the dog she hadn't met yet waking up in its kennel to bark. She had heard the front door scrape open, just under her window, Léonie's cheerful voice shouting hush, make that dog be quiet, don't wake Thérèse. Ten minutes or so ago she had heard them come upstairs together, an exaggeratedly quiet progress towards bed, caricature of tiptoe walking. What was Baptiste like to make love with? Years ago, she could admit it now: she had been tempted to find out. But then God had grabbed her and after that it was too late.

Baptiste despised her. That's what he had told Léonie all those years ago, that day when Thérèse had spied on them in the woods. She had listened to them and she had watched them. Their white legs. Then she had run off to fetch the priest.

She gave up trying to sleep, rolled over and switched on the lamp by the bed. She sat up and smoothed her fingers over the creases in her face. Even before she heard the hand fumbling at the door-handle she knew who was there. They'd always been able to pick up each other's presence. That day in the woods Léonie had known. She'd chosen her audience. She'd waited until she was sure Thérèse had arrived and was hidden behind the trees.

The door clicked open then shut. Léonie had on a grey silk nightshirt, with white piping, that just failed to cover her knees. Much fatter than they used to be, Thérèse noticed. She had a cigarette in one hand and puffed on it before she spoke. She waved it at Thérèse.

D'you mind?

Thérèse shrugged.

Not if you don't, I suppose.

Léonie's face shone with cold cream. Slabs of it laid on above her cheekbones, filling in the wrinkles like plaster of Paris. Her eyes glared through this glistening mask of white. She came across the room, picking up an ashtray on the way, and perched on the end of Thérèse's bed. She drew her legs up under her and rested her weight on one hand.

I forgot to ask you earlier on, d'you want to borrow something to wear to church tomorrow morning? I wasn't sure what clothes you've brought with you. You won't need a hat of course.

Thérèse moved against the pillow propping her back. She put up a hand to touch the scarf that wrapped her head. The nearness of Léonie's nightshirt, gleaming and loose, decided her. She pulled off the headscarf and dropped it on the quilt. She ran her fingers through her chopped hair.

Yes, she said: thanks, that might be a good idea.

The crumpled bit of cotton was blue as Léonie's tobacco smoke which hung in the air in wisps. Blue as the wallpaper behind her. Léonie looked at Thérèse's semi-scalped head. She took a deep drag of her cigarette, coughed, blinked. She screwed up her eyes, which were watering. She pointed. Thérèse reached out and switched off the bedside lamp.

Léonie said: tell me why you've come back. You've stood the life there for twenty years, why d'you suddenly want a break from it now? I don't believe what you said in your letter. You're not here for a holiday. You're up to something. Tell me what it is.

Thérèse thought: in the darkness we're equal. One married and one not, one plump and one thin, one truthful and one a liar, one who belongs and one who doesn't. It doesn't matter any more, our difference. It's all flattened out. Like wearing the habit. No bodies you have to notice. Freedom. Sisters together under the skin, made identical.

She smoothed out the headscarf and laid her hands neatly on top of it. She instructed them not to get excited and wave about. Léonie was a hump of darkness at the other end of the bed, crouched over a burning red dot. The dot lengthened, fell.

We used to sit up like this when we were young, didn't we? Thérèse said: talking. We used to tell each other everything. All our secrets.

Did we? Léonie said.

Her silky bulk rolled nearer Thérèse. She smelled of facecream and flowery scent and cigarettes. She wriggled her shoulders, shifted her legs, put one hand back under her head. With the other she stubbed out her cigarette on the invisible ashtray balanced on the dark bump of her stomach. She waited. She was at home. Thérèse thought: I haven't, I chose not to, for all those years, I had forgotten.

The pleasure of two heads, close, turned towards each other in the dark. Whispers. Certain confidences could be exchanged only in the friendly night. When you were unembarrassed, more honest. When you couldn't clearly see the other's face but knew, from the tilt of her head, that she was listening. Her mouth and warm breath nearby.

Thérèse had taken a vow of poverty all those years ago. She had chosen silence. She had stripped off language like gold necklaces, pearl rings. She had few words ready for use now. She picked some out of her meagre hoard, tossed them like jacks in her palm, threw some back.

As far as the convent's concerned I'm here on a visit to my family. We're allowed out for short holidays now you know. It's just that I never chose to take one before. I thought I'd never want to come back.

Léonie sighed. She fished in her nightshirt pocket, fumbled with her packet of cigarettes, her lighter.

I think I'm going to leave, Thérèse went on: but I haven't said anything yet.

Why? Léonie asked.

She lit a fresh cigarette and drew on it.

Thérèse lay back, limbs suddenly slack. She breathed in the smell of Léonie's body, her tobacco, her sweat. A good smell. Like that of Louis. The traces of himself he had left behind as he wandered through the house after Antoinette's death, hesitant and wistful as smoke. She curled her hands together and made a church with a steeple, a waggle of people inside. Her thumbs leant together, stubby, determined.

Oh. I don't know exactly. Something unfinished here. Something I've got to do. Something to do with what happened here during the war.

Léonie's shoulders jerked forward. Her profile tautened. The tip of her cigarette winked like a cross red eye.

She said: so you've heard about what happened to Henri's grave. I did wonder. There's going to be an enquiry of course. Lawyers down from Paris. Jewish leaders kicking up a fuss. All those journalists poking around. All the old scandals coming out. Everybody's secrets being dug up.

She puffed on her cigarette. Her mouth pursed round it. Tiny wrinkles there, in the creamy skin, radiating out.

It's no use raking up the past, she said: making people suffer all over again. They want to forget not to remember. I thought we both learned that when we were thirteen years old.

Thérèse relaxed. She felt as though she were made of water. She'd be able to sleep now if Léonie would only go away and leave her alone. She hunted for the words which would send her visitor out.

I'm writing my autobiography. I thought if I wrote down what happened when we were children it would help me to decide what it is I've got to do. But there's so much I've forgotten. You'll have to help me remember.

Léonie curled up tight at the end of the bed, like a caterpillar when you prod it with a twig.

She said: leave my childhood alone. Don't you dare take away anything more of mine.

She added in a calm voice: if you tell any more lies about the past I'll kill you.

She pushed her hair back from her face. Thérèse watched her fingers encounter a hairpin, bring it out, close over it. Wavy-legged, blunt. She herself hadn't needed to use hairpins for years but she remembered the black shininess, the ridges, the thick rounded ends. A hatpin would do better for stabbing. Or one of those special pins they'd used in the convent for securing veils to coifs. Glass-headed. Long and thin. Sharp enough to draw blood.

You always were good at making things up, Léonie said: in your version I was the sinner and you were the saint. Darling little Thérèse, everybody's pet. That's not going to change is it. Yours will be the Authorized Version of what happened won't it.

You've got to be dead before you can be canonized, Thérèse said: and in any case I never pretended I was a saint.

You're a ghoul, Léonie said: picking over what's dead and gone, what's best left undisturbed.

She clambered off the bed, straightened up.

I haven't had to see you for twenty years, she said: for twenty years I could pretend that you *were* dead.

THE PHOTOGRAPHS

When she was little, Léonie was fascinated by the family photographs hung above the bureau in the main *salon*. On to thick grey paper were stuck the pictures that composed Antoinette's view of the present and the past. Red leather gave the collection a definite edge, told where reality started. Glass kept the dust off. If she knelt on the itchy brocade of the little blue armchair, Léonie aged nine could get close to the display, mist it with her breath. She picked her relatives out, one by one.

Antoinette held your eye at the centre. She had chosen to represent herself here with a portrait taken before she became Madame Martin and was just a *mademoiselle*. Her pale hair waved back from her white oval face. She had large blue eyes, a soft round chin. Her hands were clasped in her crepe lap. She'd pasted a polite smile on to her lips, fastened the lace jabot at her throat with a cameo brooch, tucked her feet to one side. High-heeled shoes with a buttoned strap. The buttons – you could just make them out if you screwed up your eyes – were pale knobs, ivory or bone, carved into tightly furled roses. In life, when Antoinette moved, you saw she was a tall woman, long-legged, with broad shoulders and hips. As a girl she'd had red hair, down to her waist Victorine said. Her terrible experiences during the war had sapped her physically, had faded her hair prematurely to pepper and salt. She didn't bother with it after that, just scraped it into a sagging bun at the nape of her neck.

What terrible experiences? Léonie always wanted to know. But Victorine would never say. Or she'd snap: don't be stupid, the war was terrible for everybody. Except the collaborators. And we all know who *they* are.

The photograph of Thérèse showed her in her First Communion

dress, breathless under a net veil and a halo of silk lilies. She clutched her white tulle skirts with gloved hands. A silvery missal was tucked under one arm, a crystal rosary looped over the other. She did not look particularly like her mother. Her curly hair was lighter, almost blonde, and her face was broad, with a pointed chin. She had adjusted herself carefully for the camera. Blue eyes wide and upturned, the hint of a holy smile, white-shod feet turned out in a ballerina position.

Léonie always got her eyes quickly past the photo of herself. Pig-faced, she called it. Green and yellow primary-school uniform of gymslip and blouse. Unruly fair hair cut short, sticking out in frizzy lumps. Blue eyes scowling. Red-cheeked and shiny-nosed; not pretty; and knowing it.

Louis's photograph was stuck next to that of Antoinette in the centre of the fanned collection. He posed stiffly in a tight serge suit, hands on top of his stick, beret on his knee. His mild face was decorated with a brown moustache that drooped over his mouth. An urn and a palm tree sprouted behind him. He sat at the head of the table at meals, and was lord and master in everything, but the house and the farm weren't really his, Victorine had once explained. They were Antoinette and Madeleine's. Louis was only the son of a poor neighbour who managed the farm for the three girls, he'd done very well for himself, marrying in.

Madeleine, two years younger than her sister Antoinette, looked straight out at you, daring you to criticize. She had left home as fast as she could, gone off to study languages in Paris, then married a foreigner she'd met there, gone dancing with when she was supposed to be writing up her notes for class next day. An English journalist. Léonie's father. Clasping Madeleine's arm, he looked like a film star, with a little black moustache and crinkled hair sculpted shiny with brilliantine. Madeleine wore a satin dress with droopy shoulders, a white satin cap perched over one shadowy eye. Her hair was pinned up in rolls and swoops. Her cheekbones stuck out. Her mouth, painted into a cupid's bow, was laughing, eager.

Maurice wasn't in the other, later photographs. He didn't get older and fatter and duller like the other adults did. He stayed fixed as a thin handsome young man with a high forehead and a beaming smile. So full of gaiety, Madeleine always said, remembering: forever cracking jokes. When war broke out he joined up, leaving Madeleine at Blémont with her sister. She chose to stay on, through the years of the Occupation, rather than to go back to the London flat, to give

Antoinette what support she could. I felt I had to, she told Léonie: she needed me. Maurice came home on brief leaves. Léonie was conceived on one of these. She couldn't remember Maurice at all. She told her schoolfriends proudly: my daddy was killed in the war. Madeleine and Léonie were referred to by the others as *les Anglaises*. Madeleine didn't mind, Léonie was sure. Because of Maurice.

Antoinette and Madeleine's older sister had once been called Marie-Joséphine, but she had taken the name of Sœur Dosithée at the Visitation convent in Caen. The deckle-edged photo taken on the day of her profession showed her posed by the crucifix in the centre of the cloister garth. One of her hands stretched out to rest on a pair of bloodied plaster feet with a nail driven through them, thick drops of red paint dripping down. A white cardboardy wimple, thin black veil pinned on top, cut the nun's face to a triangle, black slits in its whiteness for eyes, nose, mouth. The crucifix was of stone carved into roughened tips to make it look like a hewn branch. Behind it marched raw brick cloisters, angular, with few curves.

Sœur Dosithée was the visionary of the family. She had prophesied that Thérèse's birth would be a difficult one. Later, she declared that one of her nieces would become an enclosed contemplative. Don't let it be me, Léonie always prayed.

Victorine was not represented in the group of photographs. She dusted them. She did not count as family, Antoinette explained: because she was their servant.

It was Victorine who took the picture of Thérèse and Léonie that Antoinette declared she disliked yet never got around to removing from the frame. There they stood, merry pair, arms about each other's necks, heads close, grinning at the camera, teetering on the kitchen doorstep. They wore skimpy bunched frocks, little aprons tied on over them. They looked more like sisters than cousins. Antoinette complained that Victorine had got the focus wrong. The children's faces were a smiling blur. You couldn't properly tell which was which.

THE BISCUIT TIN

*T*hérèse became known to Sœur Dosithée only through the letters that Antoinette wrote about her. Frequent letters, throughout the child's infancy and early childhood. Sœur Dosithée, perhaps breaking her vow of poverty, kept all the letters that her sister sent her charting the progress of her little niece. She died when Thérèse was ten.

Antoinette died when Thérèse was only thirteen. Thérèse respectfully sent the nuns a *faire-part*, edged in black; she knew it was the correct thing to do. Shortly afterwards she received a package from the convent in Caen. Her mother's letters, returned to serve as a memento.

Thérèse did not read them immediately. She wrapped them in a piece of pale yellow silk which she tied up with a purple ribbon, and enclosed them in a square biscuit tin which she pushed to the very back of the *buffet*, behind the piles of tablecloths and napkins. The biscuit tin had come from England, part of a Christmas parcel sent by Madeleine. It was printed with coloured pictures of the British royal family, stern in velvet cloaks with fur tops, ugly crowns jammed down over their eyebrows. The paint flaked off over the years. The greaseproof paper lining went yellow. The crumbs and the grains of sugar in the corners shrivelled to nothing. The letters, when Thérèse opened the tin again, smelled of vanilla. She was angry at the time, and she was praying for guidance as to what to do with her life. The letters answered her.

Baby is a little angel, wrote Antoinette to Sœur Dosithée: I do have to admit. I can see already that she is going to be good. Her little eyes look up at me so trustfully, and she sleeps a lot and rarely cries. I'm glad the box of salt cod reached you all safely. I'd like to send you more, but what can one do? These filthy Germans take everything.

But I'm afraid, Antoinette wrote later on to her saintly sister in the convent: I am definitely too frail. I'm too nervous, too weak still, to look after the little one properly, give her all she needs. So Rose Taillé, on the farm here, has taken her. She lost her own baby a week ago, from shock we all think, after her husband was killed, that terrible business I wrote to you about, and she still has plenty of milk. It's a miracle really. It's solved every problem. I'm paying her of course. She keeps Baby with her all the time, so that she can get on with her work while looking after her, it's simpler that way. She carries her in a sling on her back. Lucky child, to be so well cared for while others suffer so much!

Baby loves her rustic life, another letter continued to the black and white sister in Caen: she's grown into a fine healthy creature. I had a peep at her last Sunday. Not letting her see me of course. Just in case. It's better not. My only sorrow is that she's turned out so fair. We've had enough of fair-haired people here to last us a lifetime! Thank God that you've been spared what we've had to go through!

THE IVORY RING

The floor of Rose Taillé's cottage was made of beaten earth covered with lino. Dark blue, with a border of red and yellow squares. A pathway worn across it, between the fireplace, the stone sink, and the door. Lino was lovely stuff in Thérèse's opinion. In the corners of the kitchen, where it fitted badly, it could be prised up, peeled backwards, waggled to and fro until a piece cracked, broke off. Chewed, it eased aching gums: a dirty comforter; flexible chocolate. Then in the cracks between the lino strips lurked crumbs, hairs embedded in solid grease. All to be prodded, tested, gouged out. The world balanced, filthy and delicious, on the tip of her forefinger. She licked it and sucked it in. Such a good baby, Rose confirmed to Madame Martin: happy to play for hours on her own.

In the corner of the dark kitchen sat the child, crooning to herself, eating dried crusts of mud and dung fallen from people's boots as they tramped in and out. Rose found her, snatched her up, tucked her under one arm. Continued to go about opening cupboards, fetching what she needed for making pastry. Being pinioned to a warm soft body: Thérèse liked it. And the firm caress of Rose's arm on her waist. Then she was dumped on one end of the table and given a dab of butter to taste, and, soon, a lump of dough to squeeze, roll into little grey spindles on the floury table-top. She patted it. She smacked it, stabbed it. Laughed, ate it.

She knew Rose's smell, her milk and sweat, her brown skin. She knew the shape of her hips, from riding on them, and the tumbling rhythms of her high-pitched voice. Rose didn't smack her charge: too little; but she would complain at her in exasperated sing-song. Thérèse minded hardly at all; just one note in Rose's music. If the child woke and cried at night, sleepy Rose took her into the warmth of the big bed's flannel sheets, opened her nightdress to her. She'd doze off again with the little one curled like a cat between her stomach and arm.

Bliss. Feeding and being fed. Love was this milky fullness, Thérèse born a second time, into a land of plenty. And she has a good pair of lungs to her, hasn't she, Rose said to her three-year-old son Baptiste: she can scream good and proper that one can. The tearing pains of hunger, her stomach ready to fly apart and explode with raging emptiness, these did not last too long. Need was assuaged. Torture subsided as the searching mouth fastened the breast to it, gobbled, drank. Savage little pig, Rose would shout as the hard gums clamped on to her, then she'd jiggle her, pleased at the child's appetite. This one would not die. This one had been snatched back. And so Rose was patient with her fits of crying and her colic and her teething fretfulness. She walked her up and down the kitchen and sang to her. Thérèse lay over Rose's shoulder, chewing on her ivory ring.

Rose was the world, the sky that curved above you when you first took a tottering step, that held from behind your upstretched hands. She was the spoon that impatiently opened your lips and put artichoke purée between them, the arm that lowered you backwards into the tin bath, the water in which you lay and splashed and did not drown. Thérèse's first word was *Rose*, and by the time she was eighteen months old she could say *cow, apple, duck, cake, dog. Maman* was a word she had to be jogged to utter. A blue shape that swam up in the doorway.

Antoinette wore her new blue suit and white beret. Her face was anxious and sweet. A stranger. Thérèse backed away from her. Sharp movements, too pale a skin, the jut of corsets: she rejected them. Louis followed his wife into the kitchen. He'd come straight from the fields, his smell was more what the child was used to. She let him pick her up. Antoinette dropped a bundle of notes on the table for Rose.

Thérèse screamed all the way across the farmyard. She screamed for most of that night until at last she fell asleep. In just a week or so, Antoinette wrote to Sœur Dosithée: she's settled back in very well. She's already forgotten all about Rose, never speaks her name. But how spoilt she's been! She's turned out very clingy. If ever I go out of the room without her she immediately bursts into tears.

THE BABY BOOK

*L*éonie's birthday was a week after Thérèse's, in mid July, just before she and Madeleine set off for their summer holidays with the family in France. Early birthdays were preserved in snapshots: round cakes blazing in the blackness, her own clapped hands in the high chair. She couldn't really remember. When she was ten years old she discovered that she had a past. Madeleine had recorded it in the baby book.

This was shiny and square, with lambs and ribbon knots on the blue cover. Coloured pictures of curly-headed befrocked cherubs with chubby legs dotted its pages. There were headings like Weight When Born, First Stood Alone, First Word.

Aged eighteen months, Léonie read aloud: the little one could say *maman*, baby, *non*, I want, *bonjour*, cat, *maison*.

Madeleine snatched the book away and closed it.

You're not taking that to France. Don't be silly.

I wanted to show it to Thérèse, Léonie said.

She stuffed her toy fox into her duffel bag but allowed his head to peep out. She pulled the string tight, strangling him.

When do we go to France? she asked.

Madeleine threw a bundle of socks at her.

Tomorrow. For the millionth time of telling you.

The sea was Léonie's bed. A long queue of foot passengers waited to get on the overnight boat from Southampton, but the sailors helped the pretty young woman, travelling alone with her daughter, to the front, and up the swaying gangway. Two more followed with her ribbed cloth-covered trunk. Madeleine was so wide-eyed and chic in her full-skirted coat and little hat. The cheery men ran to help. She gave them her best smiles. Then the boat rocked the child. The sea heaved up and down beneath her. Arms, a lap.

The night crossing to France was like a secret. Something sweet whispered in the dark. France loomed unseen. Léonie, inserted between the crisp, tightly tucked-in sheets of her bunk, stayed awake as long as possible. She listened for the siren that marked their departure, the roar of the engines that meant their journey had truly begun. The cabin floor trembled. Madeleine's bottle of scent on the wash-stand jittered. The bunk fell down and up, down and up.

We'll be out of the Solent now, Madeleine said, yawning: into the Channel.

La Manche, it was called in French. To get at French you crossed the sea. The sound of French went up and down like waves rolling in. French was foreign when you were far away, home when you were close. Léonie only half-belonged in it, growing up in England with a dead English hero for a father and a mother disguised as an English missis with English ways. French was what Léonie forgot she could speak. Swore she could not speak. English people in the suburb where she lived despised and hated all foreigners. Wogs and wops they were called. Yids. Léonie was addressed by adults and children alike as Froggy. This term at primary school they'd started learning French. Léonie had discovered that, without ever having been taught a single rule of grammar, she spoke the language perfectly. And now the boat, tiny on the black sea, slipped her across towards it. She was hidden inside. She rode on a great crest of spittle, from one tongue, one watery taste, to another.

For as they left England so they left the English language behind. Familiar words dissolved, into wind and salt spray, ploughed back into foam, the cold dark sea in whose bottomless depths monsters swam, of no known nationality. Halfway across, as the Channel became *La Manche*, language reassembled itself, rose from the waves and became French. While Madeleine snored in the bottom bunk Léonie fought to keep awake, to know the exact moment when, in the very centre of the Channel, precisely equidistant from both shores, the walls of water and of words met, embraced wetly and closely, became each other, composed of each other's sounds. For at that moment true language was restored to her. Independent of separated words, as whole as water, it bore her along as a part of itself, a gold current that connected everything, a secret river running underground, the deep well, the source of life, a flood driving through her, salty breaker on her own beach, streams of words and non-words, voices calling out which were staccato, echoing, which promised bliss. Then the boat churned on. It abandoned English and advanced into French.

In the early morning, standing on deck with her mother, Léonie listened to men in blue jackets shouting to each other in hoarse French. That was how she knew they had arrived. Not because they had reached land, the line of tall thin houses beyond the quay, but because they had docked in French. The secret changeover in the night accomplished and left behind. One normality gone, become foreign. What had been foreign become normal.

There they were, Louis and Antoinette and Thérèse, lined up in a row. Madeleine struggled forward with her bags that the Customs man had marked with a chalk sign, into their cheek-to-cheek embraces. Léonie held on to her toy fox and stared at Thérèse. Her mother's hand on her shoulder reminded her. She gave her cousin an awkward kiss.

Antoinette surveyed her niece.

Léonie is looking quite well, she declared: but her hair has not been properly brushed.

Madeleine linked her arm into Louis's.

New beret? It's very becoming.

He laughed.

Same one you saw last year. And the year before.

Come along, Antoinette said: let's not stand about. The car's over there.

She steered them all with her umbrella, her handbag.

Louis can come back for the trunk tomorrow. Let's get you home and give you something to eat. You look starved, both of you. Don't you have proper food in England?

Léonie climbed into the back of the car after Thérèse. She'd forgotten how she liked its smell: leather, cigarettes, petrol. She thought: now I'm a foreigner again.

THE NIGHT-LIGHT

*I*n the evening, lit by parchment-shaded and gold-pillared lamps, the main *salon* lost its cold angularities and became a place to linger in. As bedtime approached, Léonie tidied herself away into a corner. She squinted at Madeleine's thin ankles, arched foot swinging a high-heeled slipper. Madeleine, now she was in France, had developed a way of sighing, bringing her hands up to clasp the back of her neck, then breathing out explosively. She gave a short, cross laugh, helped herself to another cigarette from the pink and white china box the children were forbidden to touch. Louis reached forward with his lighter then leaned back, smoothing his moustache. Antoinette sat upright, Thérèse perched cross-legged next to her chair. Antoinette's face was energetic and flushed.

Léonie was preoccupied by dread. Perhaps if she admitted she was scared of going out of the room? But Thérèse wasn't, so how could she be? If only she dared ask Madeleine to come too. Her bedroom always felt too big at night. The bed shrank. The skirting-board grew high as her waist. Grotesque bunches of fingers waggled their shadows against the wall near her face, the ceiling peeled back like a tin lid. Her room was on the first floor, at the back, opposite the top of the kitchen stairs. Léonie did not trust a house with two staircases. One carpeted and well-lit, the other narrow and steep, up which something nasty could slink in the darkness to get her. She wished the adults could realize this. But they were busy talking about religion.

But you *must* see that she says her prayers at night, Antoinette exclaimed: how else can you bring her up a good Catholic? If you don't take an interest yourself and give a good example?

Léonie watched the impatient wriggle of her mother's shoulders. In the suburb in London they went to Mass on Sundays but that was that. No point in overdoing it. That was one of Madeleine's maxims. To be applied to everything from religious observance to sweeping the kitchen floor.

Madeleine put down her magazine and her cigarette to kiss the children good night. They passed from her to Louis, who sat at the other end of the sofa reading *Le Figaro*. He stroked their hair and embraced them.

Good night, my little queen, he said to Thérèse: my little flower.

Good night, little thistle, he said to Léonie: my brown pearl.

Antoinette in her stiff-winged armchair sighed over the petticoat she was hemming.

You spoil them, going on like that.

Léonie clung to the handle of the door.

I don't want to go to bed. It's too dark outside.

Be a good girl, Madeleine warned her: run along.

Thérèse took Léonie's hand.

Come on, silly.

Up in five minutes, Antoinette called after them.

There was a low chair at the foot of Léonie's bed. Plump as a *brioche*, with twisted arms and claw legs. Antoinette sat down in it, keeping her back very straight. Everyone had haloes tonight. Downstairs Madeleine's hair flamed in the gold circle of light cast by the lamp. Up here, Antoinette's profile was faintly illumined by the night-light which floated in a saucer of water on the wash-stand by the bed. The stump of candle kept the spiky shadows at a certain distance. They leaped about in the form of imps, black baby devils.

Léonie knelt in front of Antoinette, rested clasped hands on her solid knees. She stretched out the Our Father as long as possible. How completely different it sounded in French. Softer, and grander, both at once. She got through it without a mistake. Antoinette stroked her cheek.

Very good.

Léonie asked: where will I go when I die?

You know what the answer is, Antoinette protested: to heaven, if you're good. Now jump into bed so I can tuck you in.

Léonie kept her hands outside the covers as she had been taught by the nuns at her primary school. The devils trembled towards her as though she wished for them. They opened their mouths to show her sharp tongues and teeth, ready to bite, gobble her up.

She gabbled: I don't like the dark. Dead people come in here and start talking. I don't like them. They start crying.

Antoinette's eyes flew wide open, like a doll's. She stared. Her voice was high and cross.

Really Léonie. You say the most ridiculous things. It's you that talks and starts crying. There are no dead people in this house I assure you. Dead people can't talk. They're in the cemetery, at rest. Don't be so silly.

She blew out the night-light.

Thérèse is asleep already next door. You be a good girl too and go straight to sleep.

The door shut. Antoinette's high heels tapped her away over the wooden floor of the landing, towards the front stairs.

Léonie twisted the corner of her pillowcase into a tight spiral and chewed it. Something ticked in the shadows over by the door. She tried to become flat as the sheet, to stop breathing. She listened. Now it was a shuffle, as of worn loose slippers. A slack tread. Back and forth. Back and forth. And then the voices. That cried out, and chanted, and mourned. In a language she did not want to understand.

THE SILVER CAKE-TRAY

A lane divided the back of the Martin property from the woods. The lane led to the village one way, and off towards distant farms the other. So the quickest way to get to the woods, if you were part of the Martin household, was to enter the orchard farthest from the house and climb over the vine-clad wall at its end. You hopped across the clay and stones of the lane, and *voilà*, you were there.

Victorine went first. She straddled the wall, her basket placed carefully on the big stone next to her, then hauled the little girls up and over, one after the other. Their skirts rode up about their waists, they scratched their legs, their knickers got streaked with moss. Brambles caught at them as they slithered down.

I'm bleeding, Thérèse shouted: I've got a wound.

Victorine spat on her handkerchief, mopped at the reddened knee.

Don't make such a noise. If we're very quiet we might just see a deer. You often do round here.

The three of them stood in the middle of the lane, snuffing up the keen cold air. Gnarled old apple trees on one side of them, beech trees, sloping upward, on the other. A curl of green fields on either side. The entrance to the beech wood was narrow, the end of a funnel. They waited for some long-legged creature to come stepping delicately out of the trees. Nothing. So they went in.

It was dark and quiet. No birds in here, calling out, not even the buzz of a fly, the swish of a cow's tail. Hairy beech husks mashed under their feet. Smooth brown trunks of the great trees. Sunlight lay like bits of white rag on the brown floor.

Victorine had no notion of going for walks. She said only the

English, that bizarre race, did that. You went into the fields and woods for what you needed, according to season. Kindling perhaps, or primroses, or mushrooms. Today the hunt was for blackberries, which were known to grow in profusion on the high banks of the fields beyond the woods. From them, mixed with redcurrants and blackcurrants, Victorine produced a notable conserve.

She led the way, singing as she went. A ballad about a soldier returning from war and being wooed by the king's daughter. He beat his drum under her window and she asked him to give her a rose. But he rejected her: too ugly.

Dans mon pays il y a de plus jolies, hummed and frowned Victorine, keeping them in step like the soldier: one two one two.

Suddenly she stopped.

Look. There it is. That's the place.

What? I can't see any.

Not blackberries. The place where the shrine used to be.

An outcrop of white rock from the steep hillside seemed to the children as tall as a cliff. Vivid ferns clung to its foot, where a stream curled across the little clearing. The water came from the base of the rock. It collected there in a stone hollow, fell down over moss. They dipped their fingers in.

What's a shrine? Léonie asked.

Victorine put her hands on her hips. Her small blue eyes were cheerful, contemptuous.

You're so ignorant. You come here every year for the holidays, you live amongst French people, and you still don't know what a shrine is.

She cuffed Léonie lightly on the cheek.

She is, was I mean, a very ancient saint. I don't know her name. Perhaps the Virgin. Her statue used to stand on that ledge of rock, just there above the spring. She had a long pleated dress and bare toes under it, a very young face and long curly hair, and she held a bunch of corn. Or flowers. People brought her gifts. People used to come here all the time, in those days, before the war, to ask for things. Especially for ill children to be cured. They used to leave the children's shoes at the foot of the statue, as a thanksgiving. As a sign.

Thérèse and Léonie stared at the steep wall of rock, at the grass and weeds at its foot. A makeshift altar had been built in front of the spring. A tall heap of boulders, white, somewhat tumbledown.

Then, Victorine went on: when the new priest came, our *curé* that is, he had the shrine destroyed. Rubbish he called it. He said we had to pray in church, not out in the woods. People used to come here at night at harvest festival time and pray and dance. He stopped all that.

Nothing left of the saint that the children could see. Not a stone fingernail. Not a tattered shoe. Nothing except green plants, white rocks, water. Nothing except the altar built in the heart of the wood, next to the spring.

The *curé* was a suave man, dark, with an impassive long face, a thin unsmiling mouth. His words flowed down smoothly as the black cloth of his soutane. Children spotting his tall black shape in the street ran away from him, not towards. Thérèse thought this was because he liked only clever and well-educated people. You had to grow up and get into the *lycée* to have half a chance with him. He was not like the saints you read about who had been parish priests. Not like the *curé* of Ars. Or all the others there must have been. He was more like a cardinal or a bishop, he was so grand. You could see that he would be more than a match for some small female saint with no name.

Did he smash up the statue himself? Léonie asked: or did he put her away somewhere?

I don't know, Victorine said: it was all pulled down from one day to the next, and you know it happened during the war, everything was topsy-turvy then. The statue just vanished.

She spat on the ground.

The Germans did their fair share of tearing up the woods. Using them for their filthy business.

What filthy business? Thérèse asked.

Killing people of course, Victorine said.

She pointed at the spring.

This was once a powerful place. Full of magic. Not any more.

They trooped through the sunlit darkness, keeping close together, and came out halfway up the hill on to the slope where the blackberries grew.

Do you still hate the Germans? Léonie asked.

Of course, Victorine said: when you think of what they did to people here. To Rose Taillé for example.

What did they do? asked Thérèse.

Oh, Victorine said: you're too young to understand. One day when you're older I'll tell you.

She was red in the face. She twiddled a strand of her frizzy blonde hair. She screwed up her mouth and regarded them.

Let's get on and pick blackberries.

THE CARPETS

*T*he war was a sort of bookmark which divided the pages of history. Victorine mentioned it casually all the time. Before the war we. After the war he. During the war they.

The local children just ran wild all over the place, Victorine said: I remember them riding the cows and holding cow races, oh those children had a lovely war.

Better than now, then, Thérèse said: not having to help with housework I bet.

They were dusting the main *salon*. Thérèse and Léonie did the unbreakable things, like the legs of chairs, the tops of tables, the strip of tiled floor showing between the carpet and the wall.

You can't imagine what it was like, Victorine stated: Germans everywhere. They billeted the men all over the village and even in our outbuildings here. And the officers took over the house.

She began to inspect the children's handiwork.

Haven't you ever wondered, she said to Thérèse: why your mother had these carpets put down?

Thérèse threw her duster in the air and caught it.

I couldn't care less. Can't we go and play outside now? We're finished in here.

Victorine stooped and lifted a corner of the carpet.

Look. See? The marks of the Germans' boots. All over the ground floor it used to be beautiful red tiles, spotless. Now it's all ruined, every inch.

Léonie peered at the pockmarks in the red surface. The memory of the house made visible. Scars that would never fade. The injuries of the house lived on, under the carpet which concealed them. Once you knew they were there, you could not forget.

One of the girls from the village, Victorine went on: used to come out to help me with the cleaning. In the end she took to sleeping here, it was easier. We gave her one of the little rooms upstairs, at the back.

Her glance crossed Léonie's. Her voice became casual.

Well, she got very friendly with one of the German officers billeted here. I used to see her creeping up to his room at night. Of course *he* had one of the big ones at the front.

Why? Thérèse asked: what for?

Victorine stared at her reflection held in the ornate frame of the mirror over the fireplace while her fingers dusted the china vases that flanked it.

Anyway, nowadays she runs one of the bakeries here, that one we never go into. That's why we don't go there. Didn't you know? She's very respectable nowadays. Oh yes. But we never visit her shop and she knows why. We'd rather starve than go in there.

Oh, Thérèse said: you mean a *collaborator*.

She lifted her chin.

Vive la France! Vive de Gaulle!

THE RECIPE BOOK

Victorine was juggling with potatoes, to make the little girls laugh. She could keep three in the air at once, a skill she said she taught herself after she was taken once, as a child, to the circus.

Gougère for supper, she sang out: Thérèse, find the recipe for me.

The recipe book lay on the table. Stiff blue cardboard covers, battered and cracked, pages of coarse paper yellow at the edges. Printed in wartime. The book's old-fashioned typeface, cramped and black, was as distinctive as Victorine herself in her dark dress and blue check overall, rapt lady clown with a glistening face and deft wrists.

She came, panting, to a halt. They applauded. She tossed the potatoes, hop hop hop, into the basket held by Léonie, then bowed. She tied a big red-and-white-striped drying-up cloth around each of their waists and made them kneel up to the table on chairs.

Peel the *patates* for me for the soup, she said: and I'll keep the pan of *choux* mixture for you to lick. I'll make a cake too.

French cakes, Léonie mused: aren't as good when they come out of the oven as English cakes. No currants and raisins. No icing. No hundreds and thousands or anything.

French cooking, Victorine asserted: is the best in the world!

Her blue eyes narrowed to marble chips. She pushed back a long fair curl with one hand. She whacked butter and eggs with her wooden spoon.

Suet pudding with slabs of butter and white sugar, Léonie recited: fried eggs and bacon, fish and chips, kippers, marmalade, proper tea, Eccles cakes.

Thérèse flicked a piece of muddy potato peel across the table.

Everyone knows that English food is terrible, she stated: soggy boiled vegetables in white sauce, overcooked meat, I don't know how your mother could stand it, having to go and eat stuff like that. She stopped being really French, everyone says so. The English are just heathens, aren't they Victorine?

Heathens was a word Victorine applied to foreigners. Who were not Catholics. The people in the famous circus, for example, that she was always telling them about.

Léonie frowned very hard so that she would not cry. She concentrated on her potato, gouging out its deep black eye with the serrated tip of her knife. The potato was called Thérèse.

Tell us about the circus, Thérèse said to Victorine: tell us about the costumes that shone in the dark.

Thérèse loved hearing about the padded silver suit of the terrifying and sad white clown. The pale blue tights, moulded over bulging thighs, of the male trapeze artists, that made you think about the flattened bulge between their legs. The frayed leopard skin, that left one muscled shoulder bare, of the strong-man lion tamer. Victorine perched in the darkness on a wooden bench with no back, feet dangling over the steep invisible ground. Smell of sweat and hot straw and animals. Then the toot of a trumpet and the clown with the enormous sorrowful eyes was coming at her in her ring-side seat and she wanted to run away.

The circus, Victorine began, pushing the bowl of cake mixture towards them: was run by gypsies.

She dropped her voice to a scratchy whisper.

It used to be said that the gypsies stole little children. Little curly-haired blonde children. And then killed them.

Thérèse sucked her fingers.

What!?

Yes. Just like the Jews. People used to say that the Jews liked to steal Christian children and babies. They killed them and then used their blood for baking the Passover bread.

Really?

Of course no one believes that any more. But people used to.

Thérèse said: the Church says we have to pray for the Jews to be converted to the one true faith.

Léonie was confused: Jesus was a Jew wasn't he?

Yes, silly, but then he invented Christianity, didn't he, so all the Jews were supposed to stop being Jews and be Catholics instead. Only they wouldn't. They had Jesus put to death. It was their fault, really, that Jesus was on the cross. They were as bad as the communists. You have to pray for them, that they'll repent.

Oh.

Léonie went on licking the cake mixture out of the bowl. Her Catholic primary school in the north London suburb had many Jewish pupils. When she went home to tea with them she ate delicious food. Bagels with cream cheese and smoked salmon, pumpernickel bread, gherkins, rollmops, chollah bread, pastries rich with poppyseed and cinnamon. But now she denied that memory. She ran her forefinger around the inside of the white pyrex bowl and said nothing.

A little later on she went to find her mother. Madeleine was sitting at the red and black wicker table in the little conservatory at the back of the house, pinning a paper pattern on to the green and blue paisley material she had spread out in front of her. She looked surprised to see Léonie.

Whatever are you doing indoors on such a lovely afternoon? You should be off out playing with Thérèse.

We were helping Victorine, Léonie said: anyway it's nearly supper-time.

Madeleine frowned.

You shouldn't spend so much time with her you know. You should do things on your own with Thérèse more. She's your hostess after all.

Léonie stroked the pattern with her fingertip, to flatten it. She took a silver pin and inserted it where a dart was marked with a black V and a dot. Madeleine picked up a pair of pinking shears and began to slice through the material.

Did Daddy like coming here? Léonie asked: did he like this house?

Madeleine was now absorbed in her task. She bent over the pattern, her strong fingers guiding her scissors. Her voice was no longer the fussy one she put on for ticking Léonie off. It was warmer, more amused.

Oh he loved it. He got on really well with Louis you know. They were friends, even before Louis married Antoinette. They used to sit here together for hours, smoking their pipes and chatting. They'd take their *apéritifs* in here before lunch, and their coffee afterwards.

Or Maurice would go out and help Louis on the farm. He loved Antoinette too. He understood how she needed me when war broke out and most of the men were away, he realized I wouldn't feel able to go back to England and abandon her. He said: don't worry, old girl, you've got two homes now, that's all.

The cut-out sleeve flopped neatly on to one side of the table. It had a paper lining, like a thin white shadow, fine and smooth to the touch. The paisley cloth hid underneath.

Haven't I ever told you the story about Maurice helping Louis hide all the wine? Madeleine said: that'll show you how much your father liked this place.

She spread out another section of paisley cloth and pinned another bit of pattern on to it. The second sleeve.

There's not much to tell really. It was when Paris fell and the Germans were occupying everywhere. People in the village could imagine what it would be like, the Germans taking all their supplies. So they got together and decided to hide their cider and wine so the Germans shouldn't have it. Our cellars are so big, they put it there, under a great heap of sand. Louis and Maurice and Henri Taillé worked all night, digging. Hundreds of bottles they buried. The Germans never found them. Well, once they nearly did. When Antoinette, when she ... Well. But it was all right in the end. After the war everybody got their wine and cider back. They knew Maurice had helped. They were grateful to him. They knew he loved France.

No quiver in Madeleine's voice. She snipped serenely. Her scissors took long delicate strides. The cloth fell apart as they advanced. Léonie left her to it and returned to the kitchen.

It was empty. It smelled of hot cake rising in the oven. She put her hand on the wooden knob of the kitchen table drawer. A popping wooden eye level with her chest. Like Pinocchio's nose it could shoot in and out. In here Victorine kept old butter papers, pieces of string, loose boiled sweets, old corks, red-stained, with their sweetish smell of wine. Also in here she kept the key to the cellar door. Léonie scrabbled at the back of the drawer and drew it out.

THE CELLAR KEY

*T*he cellar door was in one corner of the kitchen, near the window on the outside wall. Its paint glistened black. It was kept locked, and entry to it forbidden to the children, as Léonie knew perfectly well. Another door led into the cellar from outside in the yard, and that too was kept locked.

The cellar, being a sort of tunnel between yard and house, would have made an excellent place to play in on wet days. Too dark, too dangerous, said Antoinette: easy to cut yourself on a broken wine bottle or get your frock filthy with cobwebs and dust. Léonie had never been bothered by the prohibition; there were so many other intriguing sites for play. Now she thought: how mean grown-ups are. I'm going to see what it's like in there.

The black iron key turned easily in the lock. The door swung open inwards. A china light-switch, finger-flicked, showed her a narrow wooden staircase. She hesitated, then crept down.

The stone coolness below the house smelled of soil. She stood on a floor of trodden earth. The single light-bulb dangling on its long black cord showed her rows of iron racks. The heels of wine bottles were cold green moons she stroked as she slid past. A tall barrel had split its sides, gaped. She stopped when something soft and fluttery brushed her face. She was deeper than the house, level with worms, all the dead things that were put into the ground. Had that been a spider's web that touched her cheek just now? Where was the heap of sand? Perhaps it was time to go back upstairs.

The light went out. The door into the kitchen slammed. Léonie stood on the bottom step and clutched the metal handrail. Black water lapped her, depths she could not see into. When she opened her mouth to shout, darkness filled it, a black biscuit tasting of wine.

She was part of the shadows now. Not Léonie any more. She was dissolving, into musty air.

The door above flew open. Oblong blaze of light from the kitchen. Antoinette's legs, white and bare, black and white folds of her dress skimming her knees, her sandalled feet bound in black straps.

Her voice was shrill.

The cellar light's gone. There's someone down there. Who is it? What are you doing? Victorine! Madeleine! Come here!

Léonie turned her face upwards.

It's me, Aunt.

You gave me such a shock, Antoinette cried out: come out of there this minute do you hear?

Now that she had to leave it, the cellar was suddenly a friendly place. In the kitchen she shrank before her aunt's wrath and trembling hands.

You know it's the one thing I really can't stand, Antoinette shouted: disobedience.

Madeleine spoke from the doorway. A warning, from one grown-up to another.

Don't let yourself get into a state. She didn't realize. She doesn't know about the cellar. I told her the story about the wine, that's all. She just wanted to have a look.

Antoinette locked the cellar door and flung the key on the table.

Why don't you all just leave me alone.

THE RED SUITCASE

*A*ntoinette's suitcase was bound in scarlet cloth. She was weighed down by it. She dragged it across the Customs Hall. She had got off the boat and was looking for the way out. Léonie followed her. None of the uniformed Customs men would touch the red suitcase, let alone chalk a squiggle on the side and allow it through. Back and forth Antoinette went, ever more urgently. Léonie crept behind. Red and dangerous, that suitcase. The Customs men knew it. They'd been tipped off. A bomb inside it, timed to explode and tear them all to shreds. Red shreds of flesh. Antoinette began to run. Watched by Nazi soldiers through plate-glass doors.

Léonie's bed was stinking and wet. She sat up, crying. Already she could hear the scolding she was sure she'd get. Ten years old and you've wet the bed! Really, at your age, this is too much. She was too frightened to get out of bed and go to find Victorine. The room was full of her aunt's mad red grin.

THE SOFA

*T*he doctor's car was long and black. It crunched round on
the gravel in front of the house then sped off through the
gates scattering white stones. Madeleine shut the gates. She came
back slowly towards the house. Seeing Thérèse and Léonie watching
her from an upstairs window she straightened up, smiled, waved.

Come on, Victorine bullied: no nonsense, put that frock on and
don't argue please, Thérèse.

She screwed a wetted face flannel into a point and dug it into
Léonie's ears, then attacked her unruly hair with a hard brush. The
dresses, in cotton voile, were scratchy with starch. The children took
deep breaths, tried to shrink their shoulder-blades, as the buttons
were done up at the back. The puff sleeves were too tight under the
armpits, pinched your flesh. Crocheted white socks, crunch at heel
and toe, black patent strap shoes crammed on over them, and Léonie
and Thérèse were ready. They leered at each other, then tittupped
down the polished wood of the stairs, clutching the banisters. Soles
slippery, wanting to skate.

Mind you behave, Victorine called after them: don't give us cause
to be ashamed of you.

The ladies of the village had already arrived, and were sitting with
Antoinette in the white *salon*. This was a ground-floor room which
bulged out on the side of the house looking towards the big lawn and
the stables. Having windows in three of its walls, it was always full of
light. A severe light. A chaste light. The room was as coldly white as
death. White brocade wallpaper, white muslin at the windows, white
porcelain statues on the mantelpiece and the occasional tables, white
lace of the shawl folded across the arm of the sofa.

Antoinette reclined here, surrounded by the doctor's wife, the pharmacist's wife, the teacher's wife. All in silk frocks, gloves, hats. The hairs on the back of Thérèse's neck rose up and shouted Danger. Sombre colours. Hushed voices. Troop of old crows, she thought: coming to peck us about. Hand in hand with Léonie, she advanced, as yet unseen.

The sofa was upholstered in yellow and blue satin, shiny and tight, finished with rolled gold cord and tassels. A hard little matching satin bolster tucked in at either end. Gold claws at the end of twisted wooden legs. Antoinette did not seem comfortable. She looked as though she might slide off at any moment. The sofa merely tolerated her. Any moment it would buck, toss her, white broken heap, on to the gleaming floor.

The ladies looked up. Thérèse bounded forward, toe pointed, all smiles, ruffles, to receive pats, petting, kisses. She leaned against her mother's shoulder, stroked her hair, cheek to cheek. Léonie, sweaty-palmed, shook hands all round. Antoinette smiled, pointed.

The little girls retreated to the padded bench in the bay window. They stretched their ears across the room to hear the tut-tuts, mutterings, to decode the sighs and silences which surrounded them.

When.

If God wills.

A long remission, he thought?

Then.

So.

The white *salon* was thick with feeling. Sturdy as the white blancmange that Léonie hated and thought she had left behind in England. Now here it was in France, glutinous, gloating.

Why ever didn't you send for him before?

Working too hard for years.

Victorine came in with the tray of tea. *Tartines* of yellow sweet bread soaked pink with blackcurrant jam for the children, a slice each of set custard with a blackened skin, wrinkled and curdy. Flavoured with nutmeg. Léonie felt sick. She tugged at Thérèse's skirt. Antoinette noted this gesture, clapped her hands.

Go on children, run outside and play.

They loitered at the front of the house, at the garden corner, sharp angle of white stone, and scowled at one another. Strangers because of their clean clothes they must not tear or get dirty. Léonie the lumpish foreigner forgetting her French, hot and red-faced, scuffing the point of her shoe on the gravel. Everything she hated was white: that slice of custard just now; these little stones hard as sugared almonds at a christening; the cones of rice, curly as white hyacinths, floating in a sea of whipped egg white, that they had as a supper treat; the damask of the tablecloth that her sweaty palms would soil; the chilly marble of the fireplace in the white *salon*; the glistening pearls of tapioca that lurked at the bottom of soup. Breast cancer, she thought, was white. Whiteness of skin and bones, bandages, hospitals. All the words adults did not say.

But Thérèse liked white. She liked the words that described it: spotless, pure, immaculate. She approved of the crispness of the linen coifs of nuns, the ironed cleanness of her mother's Sunday gloves, the drift of long tulle skirts that had stirred about her on her First Communion day, the soft transparency of the veils of village brides. She was delighted when Louis called her his little snowflake, his little flower, little lily of the valley. She imagined the doctor wrapping her sick mother in white quilts, white fleeces, white blankets.

Léonie shut her eyes and frowned. She did like some white things. Yes. The sugar icing on cheap currant buns at home in England, a thick layer, that cracked then melted. She opened her eyes again, winked at Thérèse.

Let's go and play in the cellar. Victorine won't know, she's still busy dishing out the tea.

Thérèse hesitated. On a day so out of the ordinary, wearing her best summer frock, she was perhaps entitled to behave in an unusual way? She decided she would be disobedient. She crept after Léonie. They glided down the wooden stairs.

Dirty cobwebs dangled from the brick vaults arching above their heads. The wine racks were dusty. Thérèse drew her forefinger across the cool iron and traced a zigzag. Then she leaned forward and blew the dust away. She stood up very straight, stretched her arms out in front of her, shut her eyes.

Look. I'm being a sleepwalker. Like you when you were little.

The pool of light in which they stood was sharply divided from the darkness pressing up around like a stealthy animal. Léonie shivered.

More like a ghost, she whispered.

Thérèse felt her way around a barrel as tall as she was. She vanished. Léonie counted the seconds. Waiting for the thunder. This was the sound of Thérèse tripping and falling over. Léonie thrust herself into the musty blackness behind the barrel, found an arm, two arms, pulled. They tumbled back together into the lit space at the bottom of the stairs, gasping.

Look what I found, Thérèse said: right at the back by the wall. You'll never guess.

A ladylike shoe in worn red velvet, with a wonky high heel and an ankle-strap fastened with a bone button carved into the semblance of a rose.

It is isn't it? Thérèse said: one of the pair Maman's wearing in the photograph. The shoes she had when she was a young girl.

She brushed dust off the toe.

She never said she lost it.

Léonie was bored.

Well why should she? I expect she had plenty of others.

Not in the war you dolt, Thérèse said: they had to make shoes out of wood and cork, Victorine said so.

Léonie looked at her cousin with satisfaction. The bow trailed in her untidy hair, her face and arms were smudged with dust, the skirt of her dress was torn.

Thérèse had had enough. She turned towards the stairs.

We'll be in such trouble. You shouldn't have made me come down here.

But nobody bothered them when they returned to the white *salon*. The ladies had gone, and Madeleine and Louis were sitting with Antoinette in silence. They didn't seem to notice the children's dishevelment. They were very still. Staring at the empty air.

Thérèse put on a joyous smile, skipped up to the sofa to kiss her mother. Antoinette looked at the object clutched in her daughter's hand. Patches of red appeared on her cheeks like bits of worn red velvet. She seized the shoe and threw it into the fireplace.

Really. At your age you should know better than to bring rubbish into the house.

THE SACK

The children haven't noticed anything, Madeleine said: they're too young. All they think about is playing.

She was talking to Victorine in the kitchen. Léonie and Thérèse were down the other end, putting on their boots. They were getting ready to go out with Louis.

The bull had got loose from his tether. The current in the electric fence surrounding that particular field had been turned off, since the bull was made fast to a stake by a thick rope. Somehow he had worked himself free. At any moment he might trample into the road, lower his head, run at someone. Louis and the two girls set out to catch and resecure him.

He was grazing near the edge of the field, where the grass was juicy and thick. Thérèse and Léonie lay flat on their stomachs, heads well down, just where the long grass began, peeping through the stems itchy with insects. They longed to sneeze but did not dare. Very close reared the great bull. They could hear the rasp of his breath as he tossed his head against the cloud of flies that haloed it.

The soles of Louis's boots wriggled forwards. His behind, in rubbed brown corduroy, heaved and sank. His bony wrist snaked out, towards the trailing end of the bull's rope. His voice hissed back to them.

Got him!

They ran into the kitchen, shouting to Victorine.

We've been in danger. Could have been gored.

Victorine looked over their heads at Louis.

Madame's back from seeing the specialist. Doesn't sound too good, she says.

I know, Thérèse shouted: let's go and look at the kittens.

The cat had made a sort of nest in one corner of the stables. In its depths struggled small blind creatures, curled, feeble. Léonie and Thérèse knelt down in the straw. The squeak of the stable door made them turn round.

Baptiste Taillé had followed them in. He was a stocky boy of middle height, with blue eyes, a bristling crew cut, and red cheeks. His trousers, made of what looked like sacking, were chopped off at the knee, held up by a strap wound round his middle. He wore a thick jumper, and wellingtons.

He picked up a kitten by its tail and swung it to and fro in the air, laughing at its cries.

They're all going to be drowned today, he sang: are you going to come and watch?

He began to toss the kitten from hand to hand. Léonie and Thérèse pretended not to notice him. It was a way of preserving social divisions. A certain distance had to be kept. Baptiste broke the rules. He picked up a second kitten, dangled one from each hand, swung them so that they hit each other. He whistled. His bright eyes dared the girls to challenge him.

They turned their backs. Léonie caught herself feeling sorry that this had to be so. That silent disapproval had to emanate from her and Thérèse in order to prove that they were young ladies, to provoke him to further displays of cruelty. A stupid game dedicated to shoring up the notion that they did not want to play together. She gave the mother cat a final pat, sighed, put her nose in the air, and followed Thérèse out of the stable.

Eengleesh peeg, Baptiste shouted after them.

They clambered up the rickety wooden outside staircase to Louis's workshop in what had been the grooms' quarters. Here he mended chairs, weaving fresh straw into the seats, fixing wobbly legs. He regilded picture frames, glued back together broken cups and plates. Today he sat surrounded by paints and solvents, balls of string, boxes of old cotton reels and electrical parts, but he wasn't working. He was twiddling a piece of cork and sucking on his empty pipe.

The children stood on the top step and spoke to him over the half-door.

Is it true the kittens have got to be killed?

Drowned, Louis said: yes. This afternoon.

He remembered who they were. He stretched his face into a smile, lifted his hand.

Be off, little queen. I'm busy just now.

After lunch the girls hid behind the kitchen door and peered round it. Louis came from the stables with a blanket-wrapped bundle in his arms.

Chloroform, whispered Thérèse: so that they won't feel anything.

Louis upended the bundle into the rainwater-butt. That was all. The dead creatures, fished out, their fur sleek with wet, were smaller than rats. Baptiste appeared with a sack into which he scooped the corpses. Man and boy went off together in the direction of the kitchen garden.

Léonie shouted: I'm starving. How long until tea-time?

Thérèse whispered: Rose Taillé only has one eye but he's got two. He's quite normal considering.

Only one eye? Léonie asked.

She fell on a pitchfork when she was little, Thérèse said: everyone knows that. First she was blind and then when she was a bit older they fitted her with a glass eye. You can tell which one it is, it's green. Her other one's blue.

His are blue, Léonie said.

To herself she thought: I want to look at him again to see exactly what colour.

She bit delicately into her slice of bread and jam.

Of course they are, Thérèse said: everyone round here's got blue eyes. Even you, half-English.

Half-French, Léonie didn't bother reminding her. She concentrated on the face in her mind's eye, the single eye that saw in the dark and coloured things in.

THE ALTAR

W hen she married Louis, Antoinette changed the house a bit, to modernize it. She had two bathrooms put in, and she had a dressing-room built, next to her bedroom. This was a sort of passage, short, lined with cupboards. A long swivel mirror collected the light in one corner. A white sink shone at the far end, some sort of covered porcelain bucket underneath it. A green rug tousled in front of the door. Stockings and petticoats, discarded for the wash, lounged about in here, flung over the back of a carved armchair. Pink silk trimmed with tea-coloured lace, damp nylon. Smell of soap, cedarwood, camphor.

It was an un-dressing room, Thérèse thought. The place where her mother, clad in an old kimono, slumped on the low chair and held whispered conversations with Victorine. Worse even than the ladies in the white *salon*. They lowered their voices right down to the floor. They hissed, as evil as geese. Their wings flared and beat the air. Hanging about on the other side of the open door, you wanted to screech then run.

Thérèse persuaded her mother to let her change bedrooms, to take one on the floor above. She put her request prettily, asking for peace and quiet to study in, more space for books and plants. Away from certain words, from the atmosphere of dressing-rooms, was what she meant. Antoinette, anxious that her illness should not upset her daughter in any way, agreed immediately.

Thérèse spent a day rearranging her things, then invited her cousin up to take a look.

It's a bit like a chapel isn't it, Léonie said.

On the far wall, opposite the door, was a big black wooden crucifix. Underneath it, a little table bore blue candles, statues of Our Lady and the saints, and miniature vases of daisies, all arranged on a bit of old sheet with a cross painted on the front.

Léonie asked: but where's your doll? Don't you play with her any more?

Thérèse pointed. There was a shoebox at the foot of the makeshift altar. Léonie went over to have a look.

She's dead, Thérèse said: that's her there, in her coffin.

Léonie took the lid off. She folded back the quilt of cottonwool scattered with gold paper stars. The baby doll's blue glass eyes winked at her. It was naked. Its gold nylon curls had been yanked out. It was quite bald.

She's not dead, Léonie protested: not yet. Not if we operate. We might be able to save her.

She pursed her lips and looked at Thérèse.

I'd better practise on you first. Just to make sure I do it right.

In the end they took turns to be the surgeon. The patient lay on the bed to be got ready. Her body was swathed in towels, except for the gap where her vest was pulled up. The surgeon prodded the shivery flesh, searching for the tumour that must be removed. The comb-scalpel parted the patient's chest in two. It tickled, and the patient had to be shushed. The bath-sponge tumour was lifted out and dropped into the soap-dish by the bed. Then a fountain-pen needle stitched up the lips of the wound in a neat blue herringbone pattern.

Second time around they added refinements. An anaesthetic was administered by injection. The sleeping patient's eyes were bandaged, just in case she tried to anticipate what the surgeon would do next. She was gagged, and tied to the bed with the cord of Thérèse's dressing-gown. The surgeon took off her own clothes as well as the patient's.

Victorine's voice issued up from the garden below the windows, demanding to know where they were. They padded down the backstairs. The kitchen was empty. Léonie raised the heavy round lid of the range and Thérèse slid the expired doll in her shoebox into the hissing tumble of red. They waited for the space of one Hail Mary, then ran out into the yard to call for Victorine.

THE DARK GLASSES

*T*he news of Sœur Dosithée's holy and resigned death came on a black-edged card in a black-edged envelope. Joy had surrounded her final hours. Now, after her long fight against cancer, she rested in the arms of Jesus for evermore.

Louis frowned while he read this out to Madeleine and the children at lunch. He put the card down and began serving out the *œufs soubise* from the dish in front of him.

Antoinette's too ill to go to the funeral, he said: and mustn't be left. And I've far too much to do on the farm. So that's that.

Madeleine picked up her fork and began to eat. This was the sign that the children could start eating too. Léonie tucked in. *Oeufs soubise* was one of her favourite dishes. Creamy onion sauce slathered over lightly boiled eggs. She'd never caught the French trick of eating slowly, relishing the food. She gobbled. She was, she told herself in excuse, so extremely hungry.

Thérèse wasn't. She looked at her father over the top of her full plate.

Darling Papa, couldn't we go to the funeral together? You and me? She was my godmother after all.

Louis lifted his shoulders.

You're too young, little one. Little girls of ten shouldn't be thinking about dreary things like funerals.

Thérèse went and stood next to him. She rubbed her face against his sleeve. Often this made him laugh and hug her. Today he shook her off. He spoke to Madeleine.

That dreary Godforsaken convent. I went there for the clothing, because Antoinette wanted me to take photographs. But never again, God help me. I was always against her burying herself there.

Léonie swished her fork around her plate to gather up the last vestiges of *sauce mornay*.

Tante Antoinette wanted to be a nun too, didn't she? she remarked: when she was young. Before the war. She told me so. Ages ago.

Louis snapped: don't talk with your mouth full.

To console Thérèse for missing the funeral, that afternoon they played a new game. Carmelites.

We'll call it, Thérèse said: all for love.

Carmelites were brown like caramels. Carmelite hermits did not eat sweets but fasted, in their desert huts, on delicacies like fried locusts, grasshoppers, and crushed beetles. They slept on piles of old sacks in the disused pigsty, had long beards and staffs, and went barefoot. Since it was very hot they just put on a loincloth, but when they had visitors they might throw on a leopard skin to look more venerable. When wicked women called Charlottes came to tempt them the hermits cast off all their clothes and rolled naked in the patch of nettles behind the pigsty. Thérèse objected to realism at this point. She said pretending would do just as well.

Léonie played the Charlotte. She copied her costume from a film poster in the *bar-tabac* in the village. She wore her swimsuit, with a plastic mac, left open, on top of it, dark glasses, several strings of plastic popper beads, and a pair of fluffy pink mules abandoned by Victorine to their dressing-up box. She wound a lime chiffon scarf of Madeleine's around her head, and practised pouting with one hip thrust forward.

Her role was to distract the holy Thérèse, who sat reading the local newspaper inside the pigsty, and make her look up. She purred and flirted to no avail.

Very good, Thérèse conceded afterwards: just like the Devil would do.

The Devil's handmaid can never win in this game, Léonie pointed out: it's not fair.

Thérèse threw down her newspaper.

All right then. Let's play martyrs.

They sat on the floor of the pigsty catacomb, praying. They wept and clanked their chains and speculated on how it would feel to be eaten alive by the lions.

I'll be the lion, Léonie said: bags I the lion.

First she posed as a Roman centurion and did a bit of torture. It was a way of working herself up to full ferocity. She stretched Thérèse on the rack until her bones cracked, tore off her breasts with red-hot pincers, then flogged her with twigs and broke her on the wheel. Thérèse refused to stop being a Christian. Her punishment for this was to be thrown into the arena. To be torn apart by wild animals.

The first time they tried out death in the arena the Christian got infected by the general bloodlust and bit the lion. Léonie rubbed her arm, very cross.

You've got to die without making any fuss. That's the whole point.

They began again. Léonie, on all fours, shuffled towards the saint and growled. Her teeth gripped Thérèse's leg. None too gently. Thérèse rolled her eyes upwards to heaven, smiled heroically, and fell over. Léonie pawed the dust.

Too soon!

They tried once more. Now Léonie's mane stuck out crisply, the blaze of a sunflower, and her fur was yellow as bananas. She scratched herself, searching for fleas. She snarled as she leapt from her subterranean tunnel out into the sunlight, on to the bloodstained sand. She swished her thick tail. She strolled.

Thérèse lurked in the corner, kneeling, hands clasped. The lion got near enough to blow hot oniony breath into her face. The lion smiled and opened her jaws.

The martyr shrieked: I'm doing a miracle, you can't stop me.

She unfurled a palm. On it lay the silky brown square of a caramel. The lion roared. Her tongue slunk out. A rasping lick on the martyr's hand and the caramel was gone.

The lion purred. Did her trick to catch the saint who avoided becoming a martyr. Lay down on her back, rolled over, waved her paws. The saint could not resist the appeal of that spotted belly, butter-soft, that pale fur so *douce* and plush. She leaned forwards and stroked the lion. Contented, planning her sermon. Virgins made invincible by God, something like that. With a silver breastplate stuck full of arrows and the roars of the bloodthirsty pagans turned to weeping and conversion.

The lion jumped up, pounced. She batted the saint smartly on to the floor, pinned down her flailing arms and legs with her own.

I've won I've won, Léonie crowed: I've beaten you.

You haven't, Thérèse screamed: I'm better than you, I'll show you, I'll never speak to you again.

They rolled in the dust, fighting, until they were exhausted and filthy. Then side by side they lay still, heads pillowed on the pile of dressing-up clothes, bodies slack. They were sweaty, and hot. They let the warm air roll over them like water. For a long time they did not speak. Their fingers slid inside each other's clothes, over each other's skin, stroking, testing. Then further, into the little purses that must never be talked about, that they weren't supposed to know they had. They were breathless, they jumped, they shut their eyes tight.

Thérèse called it dying. The moment in the game when the martyr's soul began its slow slip away to heaven. But it was too sweet, Léonie thought: how could it be called dying, most intensively living more like.

This is what heaven's like, Thérèse said: it's like this for Aunt Dosithée all the time.

And Léonie wondered: in heaven can you have the lion also, and the soft belly, and the fight?

THE SOAP-DISH

*T*he lavatory at the far end of the yard, Victorine told the puzzled children: was the only one in the house when it was first built.

Why? Léonie asked.

I don't know, Victorine said, rolling out her pastry: but people used pots in those days didn't they. It wasn't only children who used pots, everyone did.

The little shed still smelled of those days when it had been used. Léonie loved sniffing about it. A rich and powerful odour, not unpleasant outside here in the yard where the air was already scented with manure and compost, with the melons ripening in the wire *garde-manger*, with whatever was rotting in the dustbins. A man used regularly to come and take the shit away, Victorine had explained. Well, it would go on the fields, wouldn't it? Louis, catching Léonie lifting up the mahogany flap in the seat of what looked like one of the pews in church, forbade her future entry. Then he nailed up the shed door.

Honestly Léonie, Thérèse said: you are disgusting.

She linked her arm in Louis's, and looked up at him through her eyelashes. He stroked her cheek.

Léonie did not want to watch Thérèse clamber on his knee, twist her blonde curls with one finger, ogle him. She retreated to the kitchen. She watched Victorine glance out of the window, seize a shovel and bucket, dash outside.

Baptiste Taillé had given her the signal. He winked at Léonie who pottered after her.

Two carthorses gone past, he announced: lots of good shit.

All three hurried round the side of the house and issued through the gates on to the road. Loose orange heaps, recently dropped, steaming, that bristled with straw. Very good for the vegetable garden, Léonie knew. She watched Victorine and Baptiste scoop it up. Half for the Martins, half for Baptiste's mother Rose.

Children's shit was of no use to anyone. Was dropped into a disinfected gaping hole, discreetly, behind a locked door. Must never be talked about. Only adults could do that, when they checked on your health. Léonie never needed any help to go. No suppositories for her, no thank you. If she could tell no one else she admitted to herself that she did like shit. Her own. The act.

Louis always occupied the lavatory straight after breakfast. He disappeared with his copy of *Le Figaro* and his pipe. He was not to be rushed. He was gone a fair while. It was one of his places, like his workshop, for being alone and having some quiet time to himself. Where the women couldn't get at him and talk.

The day after he'd nailed up the door of the lavatory in the yard she used the indoor one straight after him. She found the curtained casement flung open to let in a stream of sunlight and fresh air. The little room smelled of his pipe tobacco, eau de Cologne, shit. The wooden seat, when she lifted herself on to it, was still warm. She sat there, her feet on tiptoe, just reaching the black and white floor, and gazed at the glazed bumps of the linen towel hanging from a hook on the back of the door, the little wash-basin shaped like a scallop shell, the black and white edging of the tiles above. The cake of violet soap in its tin dish.

Pissing was a tremendous pleasure. Voluptuously abandoning control. Relief as the bursting bladder emptied itself, easing discomfort. Shitting was an equal delight. It was, to begin with, so varied. Some days knobs of shit as hard and beadlike as rabbit droppings fell away from her. Some days slugs or pellets. On others she watched a thick brown snake dive down between her legs. Letting it out felt so good. Shiver as the shit took over, nudged her open, swelled, dropped softly out.

She wiped herself, tossed the paper into the pan, lifted the little button-shaped plunger on the top of the tank. Water swirled into the low wide bowl. In a moment it was empty.

That was what death was like. It rushed upon you and swept you away. Your body became useless, was buried out of sight. Dug into the earth, like compost or manure. Antoinette's soul would go on, everyone promised, but what was it really, the soul? Soon Antoinette would find out whether it was true or not. Léonie picked up the wet cake of soap from the tin dish stencilled with poppies and washed her hands. She left the window open and went downstairs.

THE FRYING-PAN

*A*ntoinette gripped the thread of her life for three more years. During that time Léonie and Madeleine went on coming to France in the school holidays, just as they always had. Louis got thinner, and his hair turned grey. Thérèse began studying for her *baccalauréat*, at the *lycée* in Le Havre. Victorine was more often cross as she raced about with hoovers and dusters and brooms. But the illness at the heart of the house quickly established itself as normal. The way things were. It was hard to feel that much had really changed.

Twenty-five years later, when Thérèse and Léonie at last began to talk to each other about that time, they called it the odd summer. It dragged its feet and whimpered, it crept forward, it flinched. It was a very long summer. It began with both the girls turning thirteen. It was lightened by the presence of Rose Taillé in the house, Rose with her deep voice and her olive skin and her green glass eye.

As Antoinette grew weaker, and left her bed hardly at all, she became frightened to be left alone. It was too gloomy, she said, to lie there all by herself, she wanted to get rid of her depressing thoughts. Madeleine sat with her as much as possible, abandoning her usual household tasks. Victorine brought in Rose to help. Madeleine didn't try to organize the two of them. She let them be.

When you want some extra hands, she told them: get those girls to help.

Almost every day that summer, it seemed to Léonie, there was a hill of beans to prepare, for lunch or dinner. Rose, Victorine, Thérèse and Léonie pulled up chairs to the kitchen table and set to. The thin green beans only needed topping and tailing. Snap crack as your thumbnail bit, then the fresh green smell gushed into the air.

Other sorts of beans had to be shelled like peas, from pods that could be whitish-yellow, or cream speckled with pink. The pods were split and slit with your thumbnail, then the beans thumbed out of the silky inner case. Snugly fitted into it they were flicked out, bulky and milk-white as the pearls from Madeleine's necklace the time it broke and spilt into her plate at lunch. Pearl food. The pearls were fat rice grains you wanted to bite. The pink speckled beans looked like tiny onyx eggs.

When the pierced silver colander on three legs was full you could dig your hands into the beans and trickle their cool slipperiness between your fingers. They might be eaten for supper with a ladleful of thick sourish cream poured over them. Or they might be mixed with onion and garlic softened in butter then stewed with carrots and rosemary to go with roast lamb for lunch.

While their fingers flew in and out of the earthy heap of beans Rose and Victorine talked. They described village life to each other in intricate detail. They passed it back and forth. They crawled across their chosen ground like detectives armed with magnifying glasses. They took any subject and made it manageable. They sucked it and licked it down to size. They chewed at it until, softened, it yielded, like blubber or leather, to their understanding. They went over it repeatedly until it weakened and gave in and became part of them. Tragedy, disaster; they moulded them into small, digestible portions.

They talked, Léonie thought, as freely as though they were alone. She felt invisible and powerful. She stretched and flapped her ears, listened.

Remember how they whitewashed the pigsties before they'd let their men sleep there?

One thing you have to give the Germans, they were very clean.

Very clean, the bastards.

Very polite and correct, that officer, that day.

Those scum of *sales Boches*.

Poor Mademoiselle Antoinette.

Then I found her outside the kitchen door, crying, she'd lost her shoes what with one thing and another and she was too ashamed to come back into the house.

For a long time she wouldn't tell us.

What could we have done?

What else could she have done?

Sssh.

Thérèse, seated opposite Léonie on the other side of the table, was scornful of this kitchen gossip. Oh well, she'd say: I suppose you find it interesting because you're *English*. You're just a visitor after all.

It's different here, Léonie tried to explain: in our kitchen in London no one ever drops in for a chat. There's just the radio.

Thérèse said: I'd rather be reading a book.

But she came to the kitchen when summoned to help, and she tried not to grumble at the repetitive nature of the work and the talk. She said prayers under her breath. For the souls of the dying and the dead. You had to look very cheerful and normal while you worked so that no one would guess you were praying. It was important not to look as though you wanted people to think you were holy. That was a form of spiritual pride.

The problem was that you could never do enough. You could spend your entire life praying for the holy souls, to get them out of purgatory. If, by choosing to suffer a little, by constantly sacrificing your will in small ways, you could rescue souls, then obviously you would be a selfish brute not to. But when did you stop? How could you possibly enjoy yourself if that meant taking time off praying for the holy souls? Offer it up, people said: offer everything up, the happy times too, it's all part of praying for the holy souls.

The two girls sat together at lunch, at the far end of the table. They were allowed to speak to each other in low voices but never to interrupt an adult. The lunch-time conversation tended to be less interesting than that of Rose and Victorine in the kitchen. Further above Léonie's head. She sulked in her white crocheted cardigan and modelled tiny men from the dough of her bread. She slumped in her chair and waited to be told off.

She swore to herself that when she grew up she would not wait so long between courses. She would eat fast if she felt like it. She would put her elbows on the table, she would be allowed wine, she would read a book while she ate if she wanted to. She would eat by candlelight with an orchestra in the corner. She would lay the table her own way, not the French way, and no one would reprove her for putting the forks and spoons face up. She would talk loudly and at length and everyone would have to listen to her or they'd get no food. She would never be ill and she would live to a very old age.

THE PILLOWS

*L*éonie hated the smell in the sickroom. Warm stuffiness, overlaid with eucalyptus, the stabbing odour of disinfectant that couldn't mask that other smell that was Antoinette dying. She kept away. She put her head round the door to say good morning and good night, then ran. Her behaviour was both frowned at and tolerated. Her bad-mannered English side coming out. She wanted to go back to England, to return to school, but she couldn't. Madeleine had taken her away from school. They were staying here.

Thérèse sat by the bed. Antoinette slept with her mouth open, head dropped on to steep pillows. Gasping breaths that said: difficult, difficult. She was restless. Her hands clutched the air and each other, groped for someone who was not there. Or for something whose name Thérèse did not know. Antoinette's legs and feet twitched under the covers, would suddenly throw themselves from side to side. The self-control she exercised when awake was abandoned by her in sleep, her body breaking loose to admit her confusion. Look, I'm dying and I don't know how.

The rope of her orange-grey plait tumbled on to her shoulder. She opened her eyes and looked at Thérèse. Long and considering.

She said: it's so strange.

Then she sank back to her morphine dream. Her fingers plucked at the air until Thérèse reached out and held them in her own. Antoinette wrung her hands inside her daughter's clasp. As soon as Thérèse let go of them they flew apart and fumbled in the air again. Thérèse enclosed them once more and held on. She pulled her mother back. Antoinette opened her eyes again.

A piece of ice to suck, she whispered: that's what I want.

Thérèse held it for her, burning her fingers even as the icy water dripped over them. Soon there was a puddle in the saucer she held under Antoinette's chin. Now her lips looked a little less cracked. Still patched with blisters. They were glossed with ice.

Antoinette smiled.

You are a good girl.

Thérèse stared down at her mother's little clawlike hand. She held it gently: the arm on the end of it was so thin.

Antoinette mumbled: in the cellar, don't let him see, don't let him see me, mustn't catch, safe now?

Her eyes implored. Thérèse squeezed her hand.

You're going off again aren't you, she said: don't worry, I'm here, just let yourself float off to sleep, it's all right.

At supper the food crouched on Thérèse's plate and snarled at her. She pushed her fork into her stuffed tomato then put it down.

I'm not hungry.

If she let it, the food would jump into her mouth and swell her up to grossness. She hated the way her skirts strained at the seams, the way her thighs lolled on her chair, rubbed together when she walked. She hated her stomach which stuck out as though she were pregnant however hard she tried to suck it in. She hated her breasts. Ugly fat cow, she told herself over and over again. It's puppyfat, it's just a phase, Madeleine had hummed to her unhelpfully: I was just like that at your age.

Madeleine said now: I hope you're not going on a diet.

Louis looked up at his daughter.

My little queen's getting to be a lovely big girl. But my goodness, don't girls grow up early these days.

Thérèse stared at the bread knife. She wanted to apply it to her newly grown hips and breasts, to pare off, with quick disgusted flicks of her wrist, the fat that clung to her. She was a slim girl inexplicably encased in walls of fat. She was always hungry. And once she admitted hunger it turned into greed, she was nothing but mouth, teeth, stomach, impossible ever to stop – she was starving. In these moods she could have eaten anything. Sometimes she felt she was crunching up shards of glass, blood all over her mouth. Sometimes she thought that food was like a gag. If she ate enough she would not speak and could not cry out.

Before supper she'd held the bowl while Antoinette threw up. Long yellowish strings like egg yolk. Thérèse had stroked her back with one hand and spoken lovingly. Antoinette had collapsed back on to her pillows. Wrists thinner than a child's. Her knuckles looked so big.

Louis's voice was full of anxiety.

Eat up your supper, my little Thérèse. For my sake.

Thérèse picked up her fork. She polished off her stuffed tomato, held her plate out for more.

THE STATUE
OF THE VIRGIN

*T*hérèse lay flat on the floor, face down, hands outstretched. She lay in the shape of a cross. As still as possible. Eyelashes tickling the floor, mouth kissing its varnished whorls. She shut her eyes and concentrated on the four last things listed by the catechism: death, judgment, heaven and hell.

Don't let her burn in purgatory, dear God, let her go straight to heaven. Don't let her burn.

Madame Martin, she had heard the doctor tell Madeleine when she listened outside the door: probably only had a week to live. She might go any time.

The priest was summoned. He came wearing his purple confessor's stole and carrying the little box of sacred oils for the anointing of the dying. The bedroom door shut behind him.

But you couldn't be sure that was enough. Just in case, Thérèse performed as many acts of mortification daily as she could think of. Suppose her mother weren't conscious enough to make an Act of Perfect Contrition in the second before she died, well, she'd probably have to go to purgatory for a bit and burn. She, Thérèse, would storm heaven to make sure that didn't happen. So she jumped under the cold shower every morning. She took her coffee black, without sugar. She asked for a second helping of spinach. She allowed herself to read for no more than half an hour a day. When she sat down she didn't let herself rest against the back of the chair. Under her breath, thousands of times a day, she invoked the Holy Name of Jesus.

Clearly she heard the crackling of the flames, saw her mother's flesh scorch and blacken. She shrivelled up, fell forwards, like a paper doll. Cancer was a fire. It ate her mother away.

Thérèse did not possess a hair shirt, or a belt spiked with rusty nails, or a scourge. So she lay on the floor in the shape of a cross, and prayed.

What comforted her, when from time to time she opened her eyes and squinted upwards, was the sight of her statue of Our Lady of Lourdes. The Madonna with a heavenly look, a light veil over her fair hair, blue sash about her girlish waist, hands clasped in ecstasy and a rosary dangling from one arm. Little Bernadette was moulded at the statue's base, by a rosebush in bloom, a stream curling about its foot. A bulky shawl wrapped her head and shoulders and was crossed at her back. She prayed ardently, in rapture. In real life she'd been a poor shepherdess who lived in a dungeon and had asthma. After the visions she'd become a shepherdess of souls, leading them to Our Lady and to repentance. There were no sheep on the Martin farm. Only cows, ducks, rabbits and geese. And they certainly couldn't be called poor, living in this house.

Thérèse groaned at her wandering thoughts. She lifted her head and banged it several times on the floor.

Are you ill? What are you up to? Get up this minute.

The bedroom door was open. Madeleine stood in the doorway. She looked frightened and cross. Her arms were full of freshly ironed towels.

I was tired, Thérèse said: so I was lying down for a bit.

THE CAMP-BED

Madeleine and Victorine carted the camp-bed up the stairs to the second floor, into Thérèse's room. Léonie and Thérèse followed with bedding. They wrestled, all four, to put it up. It dated from the war. Canvas stretched over poles, on metal legs that were jointed like elbows. The poles were pushed in along canvas tunnels at the sides. The difficult bit was getting the short poles at top and bottom to fit into the others. Easy to get your finger trapped in a vicious bite between peg and hole.

There, Madeleine said, gasping: that's it. Wretched thing.

On to the taut canvas base she dumped sheets, two red blankets. She caught Thérèse's eye.

No more trouble. No more ridiculous tricks. Is that clear?

To Léonie she said: no getting up to mischief, d'you hear me?

She marched out, Victorine in tow. Their feet clumped down the stairs.

While Thérèse watched, Léonie hung her few clothes in the wardrobe. She arranged her armful of books on the shelf Thérèse had cleared for her in the corner above the camp-bed. Her diary went under the pillow, her nightdress on top.

Thérèse said: you've been put in here to spy on me. I hate you. I'll never speak to you again.

Léonie considered her nightdress. It was identical to the one Thérèse wore. Both made from remnants of terylene bought by Madeleine at a sale in Le Havre and run up by her on the black and gold sewing-machine you had to pedal like a toy car. Quite a few days it had taken Madeleine, this sewing. She was glad of it. A distraction. Something to do in the long afternoons when the house was clean, empty and hushed, and Antoinette sleeping. She gathered the wrinkly flowered stuff, pink and yellow and blue rosebuds, on to the deep yoke, adding a ruff at the low neckline, pinched the elastic into the edges of the puff sleeves, tramped her needle patiently around the enormous hem. Did this twice. The nighties were big, ankle-length. Room to be grown into, Madeleine said through her mouthful of pins: don't wriggle so, Thérèse.

They were see-through. Madeleine had not considered that. While the girls paraded upstairs, giggling at the glimmer of flesh they showed each other, Madeleine set to again. This time with glossy chintz, large blue roses on a white ground with touches of pink. Peter Pan collars, wide sleeves, blue ribbon ties. Decent. Pretty. Attired in these, the girls could come downstairs to say good night after their bath. Perfectly presentable. No ironing needed, thank God.

Antoinette approved, her blink said. They stood next to her bed and dutifully showed themselves off. But she didn't care any more about Thérèse's clothes. She'd handed over to Madeleine. She drifted off again, back to her private morphine place. Her retreat. Her room next door to death. They kissed her, one cheek each, and departed softly in their pink felt bedroom slippers.

Sitting on the edge of the camp-bed, Léonie considered how to woo Thérèse out of her silence.

Let's have a midnight feast tonight, she said: a secret party. Let's go up on the roof.

Thérèse's head jerked round: how?

To keep themselves awake they sat on the floor and told stories. The grandfather clock in the dining-room sent its notes upstairs every quarter-hour. At half-past eleven the house was so quiet they decided not to wait until midnight.

Léonie chose to use the basket Madeleine carried when she went shopping in the village. Deep, with a strong handle. She filled it from the larder and the fridge. Cold chicken. A bowl of leftover cold veal and rice, its top thick with jelly. A wedge of onion tart. Two peaches. A slice of *bleu d'Auvergne*, another of *Roquefort*. Half a packet of *biscottes*. A litre bottle of wine, glass stars around its neck, that was a third full. If someone had neglected to put it away in the *buffet* after supper, then with luck it had been forgotten and would not be missed.

Thérèse watched. It isn't really stealing, she reassured herself: I live here so I can eat the food. But she didn't believe that. She screwed up her face and whispered: you're so revoltingly fat you disgusting baboon.

Léonie shut the fridge door: right, let's go.

They crept up the back staircase to the third floor, testing each tread for creaks before stepping on it, nightclothes bunched in one hand lest they trip. Inside the first attic, Léonie had discovered, if you fumbled your way through the dusty darkness to what seemed a cupboard on the far side, you found, within this, a ladder clamped to the wall that led to a trapdoor and thence to a bit of flat roof. She went first, plucked the basket from her cousin's lifted arms, then pulled Thérèse up after her.

They sat on the little bit of flat roof above the attic skylight, behind a low parapet. Another ladder behind them led upwards, for the benefit of anyone come to check the steep lift of slates. Below them was the farm, the orchards, the fields. An owl hooted and was answered. Yellow headlights swelled and sank on the road beyond the front gates as a late car swept by. In front of them rode the moon, silver-skirted, in a flurry of dark-blue clouds.

Léonie was too excited to speak. With the penknife from her dressing-gown pocket she sawed the piece of chicken into two portions and handed one to Thérèse. Fingers greasy with lovely chicken fat, mouth attacking the crisp salty skin, the flesh scented with maize and herbs. Thérèse poured a large plastic glassful each of red wine. At supper, now they were thirteen, they were allowed one tumbler, well watered. Neat, the wine made them choke. They gasped and sat back, determined to like it. They made sandwiches of Roquefort and sliced peach. The cold veal, meat jelly and rice, scooped up with their fingers, was one of the best things, they agreed, they'd ever eaten. Léonie licked Thérèse's fingers to see if they tasted the same as her own. They chucked the peach stones over the parapet so that peach trees would grow in the garden next year and surprise everyone.

Now the night was cool. They'd been sitting still for too long. The stars sprang out, pressed themselves at their faces, as a wind blew up and chased away the clouds below the moon. So bright, so indifferent, that moon. Inside herself, as she looked at it, Thérèse felt sour and queer.

She whispered: I want to go back in.

Léonie climbed into bed beside her.

Where does it hurt?

Thérèse pointed at her stomach, lay back. Léonie's hand rubbed up and down, kneaded, caressed. Smooth strokes along the cool skin. Her hand had a mouth and could talk. Be still, I'll take care of you.

Thérèse sat up and fumbled for the light-switch that dangled from a cord beside the bed. She brought her fingers up from under the sheets and stared at them. Bright red.

She said: it must be what they told us about. That thing women get. When you can't go swimming.

Léonie was awed. The blood was thin and clear. A lot of it. Trust Thérèse to get hers first. It wasn't fair.

She scrambled out of bed.

Wait there, I'll go and fetch someone.

Thérèse sounded frightened.

Hurry up then.

Madeleine's room was empty. There was a light under Antoinette's door. Léonie peered in. Antoinette seemed to be asleep. Louis and Madeleine were slumped on the sofa by the fireplace. Louis dozed, his head on Madeleine's shoulder. Her deepset eyes stared in front of her as though she was thinking of somewhere far away.

THE COFFEE BOWLS

*L*ouis looked as though he'd just got up off the ground after being knocked out in a fight. Grief had swung at him and given him two red eyes. He sagged inside his best grey suit, and his black armband looked like a bandage. He had two fresh shaving scars on his chin which his fingers kept wandering up to touch. The suit removed him from what they were all trying to pretend was a normal breakfast. Léonie, used to him clad in blue jacket and brown corduroy trousers, didn't feel able to kiss him good morning. He didn't notice her lack of salute. He stared at the tablecloth while Madeleine poured coffee into his big cup. This morning he didn't dip his bread and butter into it, munch and gulp, as usual. He just stared at the tablecloth. Léonie tucked herself into a chair at the far end of the table, next to the silent Thérèse, who wasn't eating either. She broke off a piece of *baguette*, spread it with butter and jam, stuffed it into her mouth.

Victorine, Rose and Madeleine were all in black. They stood over Louis.

All right then? It's time to go. The cars have arrived.

Thérèse and Léonie watched them depart. They crouched on the windowseat of the little white *salon*, face pressed against the cold glass, misting it. Louis, walking out to the long black car, was a sack of tears. You could see he'd stuck invisible tape over his mouth so as not to cry. He had forbidden the two girls to attend the Requiem Mass because he said it would upset them too much.

The two black cars pulled out of the gates, round the corner, and were gone. Léonie and Thérèse knelt down on the parquet floor. Eyes shut, hands clasped. They recited the *De Profundis* together, dividing the lines between them. Out of the depths have I cried to thee O Lord.

Lord, hear my voice. And let thine ears be attentive. To the voice of my supplication. If thou O Lord shalt observe iniquities. Lord who shall endure it?

They couldn't remember any more. They left it there, and went back to the breakfast table, to their unfinished bowls of *café au lait*. The coffee was cold, with skin on it.

Léonie was bursting with English words. She ran upstairs to the bathroom, covered her head with a towel and spoke to the cold white wall.

I'm glad she's dead. She had to die. She took too long dying. I'm glad she's dead.

The house was very still. It listened to her. It was making up its mind what to reply. The bath-towel over her head was warm and dry on her face. She leaned her ear against the wall.

THE BREAD-BASKET

*T*hérèse no longer shared the first job of the day with her cousin. Léonie went alone, now, to fetch the bread from the baker's in the village square. On her return she laid the cloth, collected the knives and plates, sounded the gong for breakfast. Thérèse was let off these tasks because she was in mourning. She slumped in bed, miserable and full of headache.

Poor child, Madeleine said: no wonder.

Thérèse had not once cried in public for her mother. Louis wept openly and could not be comforted. Not with caresses, not with sweets.

Leave him be, for the moment, Madeleine advised: leave him alone and he'll be all right.

Two days since the funeral. Léonie was delighted to get out of the house. She shut the kitchen door behind her, turned to study the strip of seaweed nailed there, to check the weather. It suggested wet. It was right. As she emerged into the yard fine rain dampened her face. The air smelled of salt and the sky was grey.

She sauntered around the side of the house, hands in the pockets of her shorts, trod over the white gravel to the gates. She heard a thin crowing of cocks. Her bare feet slipped in her sandals, which were already wet, and her cotton shirt felt chilly. Too much bother to fetch a raincoat. She went on out to the main road.

The ditch on her left swirled with rainwater. The bank above it was a tangled slope of late-flowering mallow and campion, bright purple-pink in the long grass. On her right the green meadow was full of cows. Every so often there was a gap in the bank of beech trees that guarded the farm from wind and storms, a muddy track between red brick gateposts affording entry for tractors into the farm lands, access to the half-timbered cottages where the farm workers and their families lived. Already the labourers' wives were returning from the village, long loaves tucked under their arms. Some rode ancient and solid bicycles. Others trudged along in wellingtons, a bulging canvas bag in each hand. Léonie knew them all by sight. She greeted each one.

The road wound away from the Martin farm into the outskirts of the village. Léonie plodded between small houses that leaned together. Through their open doors she caught flashes of patterned lino floor, a corner of tablecloth, a chair leg. Voices inside called out, responded. She went on, past the blacksmith's, past the corrugated-iron public lavatory on the corner, plastered with faded posters that peeled and flapped, across the road, through the stepped gap between two old houses whose lath and plaster upper storeys almost touched overhead, and into the little square.

She walked very slowly across it. She told herself she would not be shy, she would not blush when addressed as *la petite Anglaise*, she would not mind having her fluency admiringly remarked upon, she would not care that everyone in the shop would turn round and stare at her, the foreigner. Today would be different.

The two bakeries stood side by side. Almost identical, if you had not been brought up by Victorine to know that one was good and the other bad: both had wide shop windows displaying shelves of apple tarts, turnovers, puffs; striped awnings above; tiled steps.

Léonie stared at the two shops and came to a decision. She would go into the bad woman's shop. The collaborator's shop. Just to see what it was like. Surely nobody at home would notice if the bread, just once, tasted a bit different?

She pushed open the glass door, muttered good morning, and took her place in the queue. She couldn't believe that she wasn't in the baker's next door. Same list of icecream flavours hung on the wall and bowl of aniseed lollipops on the counter, same gilt baskets of *croissants* and racks like umbrella stands packed with tall loaves. The woman in the grey overall serving customers looked just like anyone else. She snatched up a square of tissue paper, deftly swung and twisted it round a fat *brioche*.

Léonie bought two *baguettes*. The shop-woman smiled at her and asked after the bereaved family. Léonie felt her cheeks go red. She gabbled something polite and slunk out of the door, just remembering in time to bid everybody goodbye.

She slung her long loaves over her shoulder, a bread rifle, cupping its warm heel in her joined palms. She turned towards the shallow stone steps leading out of the square.

Baptiste, four other boys behind him, blocked her path. Sweat flowed from Léonie's armpits down to her waist.

Eengleesh peeg, Baptiste yelled at her.

The boys whistled. Léonie wheeled, scrambled back past the baker's, and fled along the boulevard edged with limes that led to the church and the walled cemetery, to the lane beyond.

The boys jeered as she ran away. She let herself glance back. They'd vanished. And she still had the bread, clutched in her arms. Fear fell off her like a jacket. Her heartbeat slackened.

The drizzle had stopped. Sun shone on water. She slithered along the muddy ruts of the overgrown lane. Getting her sandals filthy but she didn't care. Delicious, the coolness of mud between her toes. Brambles hooked her shorts, unloaded raindrops all over her feet. Ferns of brilliant green slapped her legs. She picked one, hoisting the bread under one arm, and swished it over her shoulder at the swarm of cattle flies that buzzed there.

The lane was deserted, quiet. She remembered Victorine saying hardly anyone used it any more. It was a much longer way back than the road. She would be late, even if she stopped dawdling and got a move on. Her pace slowed even more as she thought of the house dark and sour with grief. And it would be her fault that breakfast would be late. She'd get a scolding from Victorine and from Madeleine as well most likely.

The strap of one of her sandals had worked itself loose. She stopped, shook her foot experimentally. The sandal flew off. At the same moment Baptiste and his gang of boys ran whooping round the corner.

Boys behind, the woods in front. Léonie pelted down the lane, scattering loaves. Freed of her burden she was fleet. She leapt over the ditch opposite the Martins' orchard wall and hurled herself into the undergrowth. The woods received her, closed over and around her, dense green water.

They hadn't followed her in. Jeering laughter, then their voices faded. Léonie sat up, rubbing her elbows. Her legs were scratched and smarting. Her foot, when she explored it with her fingers, had a couple of thorns stuck in it and was bleeding. Now she'd be in extra trouble for losing the sandal. And the bread. Did she dare go back to look for it? Suppose the boys were hiding, waiting for her to re-emerge?

She got up and limped forward. She was in a little clearing, in the centre of which was a tall heap of large stones. Behind it was a small white cliff, the bubble of water. She paused. Memory of a basket to be filled with blackberries. Victorine's tale of . . . she couldn't quite remember what.

She stood and shivered. It had begun to rain again. She hovered, not knowing what to do, afraid to start crying here all by herself.

Something like a rough finger stroked the back of her neck. Her head jerked up. Then she saw it. Saw the fine rainy air become solid and golden and red, form itself into the shape of a living and breathing woman.

Later, when she blurted out to Victorine what she had seen, when she tried to describe it, she struggled with inadequate words. Under Victorine's mocking questioning she understood that she had betrayed her vision by mentioning it. Its red and gold brilliance sank into the darkness of her imagination like a firework blazing then fading in the black night sky. All she had left to clutch at was the memory of how she had felt.

Something outside her, mysterious and huge, put out a kindly exploring hand and touched her. Something was restored to her which she had lost and believed she would never find again. The deepest pleasure she had ever known possessed her. It started in her toes and across her shoulders and squirmed through her, aching, sweet.

Then she remembered it. A language she once knew but had forgotten about, forgotten ever hearing, forgotten she could speak. Deeper than English or French; not foreign; her own. She had heard it spoken long ago. She heard it now, at first far off, thin gold, then close, warm. The secret language, the underground stream that forced through her like a river, that rose and danced inside her like the pulling jet of a fountain, that wetted her face and hands like fine spray, that joined her back to what she had lost, to something she had once intimately known, that she could hardly believe would always be there as it was now, which waited for her and called her by her name.

Time stilled, and suspended itself. In the cool drizzle. Then, with a jerk, the world went on again.

Victorine and the others were interested solely in what she claimed to have seen. Léonie tried to tell them. It came out all confused.

The red lady. The golden woman in red. She swam up slowly. She developed, like a photograph. She composed herself, a red and gold figure on a red ground.

She referred to the apparition as *that person*. It seemed to her polite to do so. Also there was no other way to express her sense of something having arrived from somewhere else, something normally invisible to the eye choosing to put on a human form. It was Victorine, listening with one ear in the kitchen with the others while she sawed a *baguette* into chunks, who laughed and said *Madame la sainte Vierge* I suppose.

Usually when she got home with the bread Léonie dumped it on the kitchen table. Then she opened the bread drawer of the dresser, took out the bread knife and the oval basket of plaited straw with its red check cotton lining. She would cut up yesterday's leftover bread, staling now but to the taste of Madeleine, and carry that and the new *baguette* along the corridor to the dining-room. Then she would open the doors of the *buffet* and take out the tablecloth.

This morning she was in another of her daydreams, it looked like to the exasperated Victorine. There she was standing in front of the *buffet* with her eyes half-closed and no sign of the table being laid. Well after half-past eight and that poor man upstairs needing his breakfast.

Victorine was confused by the tale Baptiste had told her just now when he and his mother turned up at the back door with Léonie's sandal and an armful of bread. Was it true? she demanded of the silly girl: that she'd run away from the boys when they were only trying to be friendly?

She intended to restore discipline. She took Léonie into the kitchen, where Rose and Baptiste waited. How small and cowed he looked next to his mother. That cheered Léonie up.

Victorine put Léonie on to a chair, the bread on to a board, the knife to the crust.

So. What happened to make you so late back? Tell me the truth, mind.

Thérèse appeared in the doorway. She fingered the edge of her dressing-gown. She pouted.

Oh. I just came to see if the coffee was ready for me to take up to Papa.

Rose gave Baptiste's earlobe a hard pinch. His cheeks were very red. Both girls quickly turned their faces away, just in case he would want to take revenge on them later for having witnessed his humiliation.

Rose said: was he bullying you? Because if so I'll beat the hide off him, I've told him so, he's not too big to be beaten and if Monsieur Martin won't do it I will.

Léonie said very fast: what happened was I saw this person all in red.

Victorine laughed.

A person in red. Some excuse. Why not simply admit it, that you were dawdling again. Tell us her name then.

Léonie insisted, watching the blade fall quickly through the bread, that she did not know the person's name.

Well then, retorted her amused audience: you had better find it out hadn't you?

It must have been someone from the village, Rose said: who else would be walking in the woods at that hour? The Parisians only come here for walks at weekends.

Léonie leaned her head on her hand, drew patterns with one finger in the litter of crumbs around the breadboard. Victorine took the kettle off the flame, poured a stream of boiling water into the top of the mottled blue enamel coffee-pot. A cloud of steam arose, the perfume of coffee.

Was she beautiful? Thérèse asked.

Yes, Léonie said.

As beautiful, Victorine asked: as Marie Guérin? Who had ridden as village queen on a flower-hung cart only the previous week in the procession to celebrate the feast of the Assumption.

Far more beautiful, replied Léonie. Unsuccessfully hiding her scorn of Victorine's own style of beauty: frizzy blonde hair and small blue eyes, plucked eyebrows and plump white calves, big feet crammed into white winkle-pickers.

So what did she look like then? demanded Victorine. Glancing with irritation at the cocky girl who wasn't even properly French but a *bourgeoise* English snob with no clue about what was what.

She, that person, had a wide mouth, with plump lips, like cushions. Dark eyes under feathery black brows. A lot of black hair that curled down her back. She was very young. Not fat but not thin. And everything about her, her long nightdress and the mist she was held in, was so golden-red that even the dark gold skin of her lovely face had a reddish tinge to it. As though she were made of fire. And she had yellow stars around her head.

She was coloured? Victorine roared with sorrowful mirth: oh what a story, well that certainly cuts out the Blessed Virgin.

She scooped up coffee-pot, bread-basket, jam-pots, Camembert, on to the tin tray, and made for the door. She shot her diagnosis over her shoulder. Indistinct rumble of words as the door swung shut.

Just an excuse. Or your imagination. Overtired. Staying awake too late chatting to poor Thérèse.

Rose said: suppose it *was* the Virgin? Isn't that exactly where the old shrine used to be, in those woods?

Thérèse laughed.

How could it possibly be Our Lady! She only wears blue. She's been making it up.

Baptiste flicked a look at Léonie. Comrades. They were not going to give each other away. Then he went on gazing at Thérèse, voluptuous in flowered chintz and blue ribbons.

Léonie picked up a fistful of knives and trailed after Victorine. She promised herself that she would never mention the lady again.

THE QUIMPER DISH

The room was too warm. It smelled of Thérèse's stale breath and sweat. Sour, sweetish. Léonie lowered herself on to the chair beside the bed, her magazine on her lap. She tried not to look at the glass on the pink marble top of the wash-stand, empty, a sticky red stain at the bottom. A fly circled its smeared rim.

Thérèse's face glistened. Her hair flopped on the pillow. This morning she was just a limp nightdress that needed washing. Last night she'd tried to toss the covers off, then cried weakly, tears leaking down the sides of her nose on to the sheet. Léonie hadn't been able to hush her.

No one could help Thérèse. She turned her head away and refused to recognize the women who hung over her, imploring. Thérèse, please eat. You must eat. Thérèse wielded great power in her illness. Léonie knew it. The doctor, flustered, did not. A chill, he suggested, and then: influenza. A fever. Which took Thérèse by the throat and shook her, rattled her speechless, dumped her in bed. A nervous collapse. Yes, that was true, Léonie thought: but what they all refused to see was the willpower, the rage. How she lay there, the focus of their anxious attention, and rejected them. They called it being ill. How long could that game go on?

Léonie could not say this to anyone. A criticism which would hurt. She sat still and said nothing. Thérèse was scared to be left alone. She whispered that the Devil hid behind the curtains, a red devil with a feathery red tail. Her fretfulness eased if someone stayed near her, in view. She got her way. Léonie hunched on the bedside chair and lapped up comics, while Thérèse dozed.

Léonie still could not let herself cry for her aunt. She noted that there was now an absence, but got no farther. She twisted the comic into a tube on her lap and clenched it like a truncheon. Thérèse opened her eyes.

Calmly Léonie unrolled her weapon and smoothed it over her knees.

She said: I'll have to go downstairs in a minute. I've got to lay the table for lunch.

Thérèse took this in. Her eyes still sluggish but indicating: go on.

There's no one to help me at the moment, Léonie added: so I have to get all the china out of the *bonnetière* all by myself. The Quimper dish too of course.

She stood up.

See you, then.

Five minutes later Léonie walked carefully down the stone-flagged passage into the kitchen. She carried the Quimper dish on her upturned hands. They sank under its cool weight. She set it down on the kitchen table, stroked it with one finger. A big dish, roughly oblong in shape, with rounded shoulders. Its thickness and heaviness were emphasized by the bold strokes of its painted decoration, dark orange, dark pink, and navy blue. In its centre a squat Breton countrywoman in white bonnet and striped blue gown planted her saboted feet on a clump of vivid grass. The glazed surface of the dish was a network of fine cracks. Its two handles, flattened, curled like pigs' ears, were striped in yellow and blue.

Antoinette had loved this dish, had used it every day for serving the fruit, piled on vine leaves, that ended the *déjeuner*. Thérèse and Léonie loved it too, quarrelling over whose turn it was to load it with grapes and plums, arranged in blue and green pyramids, and carry it in.

Now that Thérèse was ill in bed, Léonie could handle the Quimper dish every day. Now that Antoinette was dead, there was no one to repeat to her to be careful, not to drop it, to try at least to walk like a lady, not to plonk it down like that.

Léonie went to the orchard to pick some vine leaves. The vine clawed its way up the wall at the end. It dragged a train of pointed green and scarlet leaves. Ornamental, Victorine always said: planted for no good reason. The grapes it produced were small and hard, inedible. How could it be otherwise, in this northern climate with its rain and storms? It just proved how Monsieur Martin, with his jumped-up-gentleman's fancies, was not a real farmer at all. Not as she, Victorine, the daughter of proper peasants, understood that word.

Perhaps, Léonie thought: Louis simply liked the colours of the vine's leaves, which turned, as autumn deepened, to a fine flare of pure red. She stood, indolent, in the wild grass of the orchard. It was almost lunch-time, but the sun on her face stroked her into lingering, into staying still. A few yellow leaves lay at her feet. The trees had begun to loosen themselves of leaves as they had of golden pears, rough-skinned and scarred, a little while before. Léonie saw a dropped pear rotting in the grass, bruised amber, its creamy flesh exposed, its grainy core.

Without thinking about it she was climbing over the wall. She hopped across the lane and the ditch, and entered the woods. Wandered along the path that led to the little clearing.

She startled fully awake, alert. That touch again, its velvet insistence. As though some enormous beast nuzzled her then picked her up in its mouth by the scruff of her neck. She dangled in free air, then was put down. She closed her eyes against the play of gold and green light. Reopened them.

The lady, yes, she certainly was a woman, stood barefoot on top of the white outcrop of rock above the spring. She held an overhanging branch with one hand, as though to steady herself, and put up the other in a gesture of greeting. She smiled. Summoned Léonie with that look of interest and tenderness. Drew her, as surely as if she had her on a string, unresisting, across the grass.

Thérèse tossed in bed. For some reason she found herself obsessed with the idea that she should get up to lay the table. To help Léonie. She was helping no one lying here. In fact causing them extra trouble, extra work. She had offered up her illness for her mother's soul. And her willingness to suffer more if need be. Was that enough? But could she do more when she felt so weak?

Victorine shoved her out of her worries, opening the bedroom door without knocking and clattering in.

Oh. Isn't Léonie here then? Where's she got to I'd like to know? I need her to go and fetch the fruit from the *grenier* and then there's the table to lay and I don't know what.

Thérèse sat up in bed.

I'll go and see what she's up to, she told Victorine: don't worry, I'll find her.

Victorine opened her mouth. Thérèse jumped out of bed and hurled on some clothes. She felt capable and important. She hurried out of the room, before the astonished Victorine had completed her first sentence of protest.

Thérèse was afraid of the *grenier* where the fruit was kept. It was a high little barn on wooden legs, half-timbered and thatched, reached by a rickety wooden ladder. It was on the far side of the yard, opposite the kitchen door. Between the wooden legs Louis had built chicken coops. Thérèse hated their smell. The *grenier* above them was so dark that, stumbling across the floor, she was always afraid that it had rotted away into gaping holes. Through these she would fall into the muddy embrace, dirty with droppings, of the chicken coop below. Hens had horrible faces close to. They wanted to peck you all over, out of sheer spite. If she had Léonie with her it wouldn't be so bad. So she made for the orchard first.

She sped down the little path leading between the long vegetable beds of the kitchen-garden. How good to run, her legs wobbly at first but then miraculously able to move easily and fast. The sandy path flowed towards and under her. Tennis shoes went *toc-toc-toc*. She galloped past the rabbit hutches, the ducks swaying towards the pond. She leaned against the wooden door of the orchard, which Léonie had left slightly ajar, and put a hand to the stitch in her side. Then she pushed it wider open and went through it, calling out her cousin's name.

Léonie was not in the orchard. Thérèse looked at the red-tinged green brilliance of the spreadeagled vine. Then she understood. She ran to the wall and began to climb.

When she got to the little clearing she halted, seeing Léonie there on her knees, looking up at the outcrop of rock. Then she too knelt down.

THE DUSTPAN

*T*he two girls walked back down the salmon-coloured path towards the house, each with a bouquet of vine leaves. On one side of them was a sprawl of turquoise cabbages, frilly and tight-waisted, ready to bolt. On the other, the big green umbrellas of the courgette plants, the orange swell of pumpkins. They did not speak. Léonie ran up the stairs to the *grenier* and reappeared holding a basket of plums. They crossed the yard and reached the kitchen door. Thérèse put out her hand and opened it.

The Quimper dish lay in pieces upon the floor. Violence measured the distance of one fragment from another. Painted jigsaw bits. The Breton lady had been dismembered. Her head lay near a table-leg. Her flower-clasping hands rested at the foot of the stove.

Madeleine and Victorine awaited them.

The voices all jumped out at once.

I didn't do it. It's a miracle. Whatever are you doing out of bed? Heavens above. Just look at you. You're supposed to be ill.

Thérèse looked at the pale Léonie.

I did it, she said in a clear voice: I heard someone calling me so I got up and came downstairs. The voice was calling from outside. I ran through the kitchen. The dish was on the edge of the table. I knocked it off as I ran past. It was an accident. I'm sorry.

Heroic Thérèse, standing up straight to make her confession with shining eyes, await due punishment.

Who called you? Madeleine asked: Victorine? Léonie?

Thérèse blushed pink. She trembled. But she stood up as eager as Joan of Arc before the judges at her infamous trial.

No, it was neither of them. Something forced me to go to the orchard. So I went. The voice called me to go there. And then. It was a miracle! Aunt, look, I'm cured. It was Our Lady.

Madeleine hesitated. Her hand twitched on the rolled edge of the black silk scarf about her neck, clearly longed to rise and slap someone.

What's the point of all this fuss? she said at last: what's done is done. I'm glad you're feeling better, Thérèse. It's much better you should be up, not brooding in bed. So come along then. You can join us for lunch.

Aunt, Thérèse whispered: it was, the lady in the woods I mean, when I got there, I saw her. It was the Virgin Mary. Just like –

Victorine had become busy with dustpan and brush. Madeleine interrupted Thérèse with a sharp cry.

No, *imbécile*, pick them up piece by piece. Just in case it's worth mending. No, with your hands, not with the dustpan.

Victorine's face went bright red. Her voice was muffled when she crawled under the oilcloth-covered table to search for Quimper bits.

So wasn't she black, then? Not the same one Miss Léonie saw?

Madeleine stiffened and frowned. But Thérèse recited happily.

She had on a long blue dress. Her hair, which was long and fair, was almost entirely covered by her white veil. Her hands were clasped, and she carried a crystal rosary over one arm. Her feet were bare, and there was a golden rose resting on the toes of each one.

Léonie could see her mother making a big effort not to lose her temper.

Yes, Thérèse, just like the statue at the side of your bed. You made it up, didn't you? Your imagination. You and Léonie, what a pair. You've been ill, very feverish, so we'll say no more about it.

Thérèse flung her arms wide and broke into sobs.

I want my mummy and she's dead!

She clutched Madeleine around the waist. Her aunt melted, patted her.

Poor child, poor child.

Léonie lifted her sleeve and wiped her nose on it. Just to test whether anyone was watching her. They weren't. She bent down and picked out a fragment of Quimper from the dustpan. The joined painted hands that held flowers. Then she slid out into the hall, fist clenched over the treasure in her pocket. She seized the black leather strap dangling near the hall mirror and beat the gong for lunch. Then she ran upstairs, to put the piece of Quimper in a safe hiding-place.

She tackled Thérèse in the bath that night. Her cousin lay under a quilt of white bubbles thick as fur. She had drawn it up to her chin. Her toes poked out, and her knees. Léonie perched on the cold wet edge of the white bath and leaned forwards.

Why did you say it was Our Lady we saw? How did you know? Thérèse smiled at the taps.

She told me. I asked her her name just in case it was the Devil in disguise and she told me who she was.

She turned her head and studied Léonie. Gave a wondering smile which made Léonie want to hit her.

Didn't you hear her? I did, loud and clear.

Léonie prodded the foam with one finger. She longed to say: you're lying, you made the whole thing up so you wouldn't get scolded for breaking the dish.

She said: she didn't say a word to me. It wasn't about talking. Not that sort anyway.

She's going to come back, Thérèse said: she told me so. I'll know when. I'll just get the feeling that I've got to go to the woods. You can come with me if you like.

She glanced at Léonie from under her eyelashes.

Would you go now please? I'm going to get out. Oh, just hand me my towel would you? Thanks.

THE ORANGES

Counting could be done by means of magpies. When you were in England. The rhyme went one for sorrow, two for joy. That made you anxious to see two. Léonie's problem was that she could not count. Not these simple numbers. When did one magpie become part of two? If you spotted a smart black-and-white magpie in a field, that was certainly one, but if, when you'd walked into the next field, you saw another, was that two or another one? How much time, spent in climbing over stiles and so on, had to elapse before you could proclaim one, and then one, rather than two? How many fields, hedges and stiles were needed, what thickness thereof, to separate one from getting mixed into two?

Two was an odd word anyway. It did not express twoness. It was as short, round and compact as one. Léonie's formula was: one magpie in the same field as another magpie, both in view at once, makes two magpies. She preferred saying one-and-one to two. She knew what she meant. Two was blurry and made her anxious. She did not have this problem with fields because they had names and did not need counting. Similarly with the cows on the farm. If magpies had names all would be well. Her joy perched on trees above her head, laughed at her, flew away.

She sat on the kitchen doorstep, knees wide apart, frowning. She was juggling with two oranges. They whirled through the air in front of her, an oval streak of orange. One. Then she made them slow down, and two oranges again spun between her hands.

One red lady. One blue.

One? Or two?

THE GREEN SCARF

*L*éonie and Thérèse gave the scarf jointly to Victorine on her birthday. A square of thin green wool scattered with small paisley shapes in yellow and red. Victorine protested that she did not need a new scarf and that green was not her colour. She said she'd rather have had some lilac bathsalts, the sort that crumpled to silk in the water. A good soak in fragrant steam. To ease her aching legs. In the end she yielded, declared that she would wear their gift, tucked inside her raincoat. Her old scarf, purple rayon printed with black flowers, she would demote to second-best.

Now the green scarf would become part of Victorine. Like her blue overall for cooking, her little gold earrings, her grey tweed overcoat for winter, her beige mac that doubled as her coat in summer. She took care of her things, she made them last. She folded her jumpers around sheets of tissue paper after ironing so that they wouldn't crease on the shelf. She hung old cotton sheets around her Sunday dress, her pleated terylene skirt. She slapped, brushed, shook, mended, darned. She kept things in good repair. She made sure that they went on being there. She saved them. She hadn't been able to save Antoinette.

As it's my birthday, Victorine announced: I'm going to visit Rose. I'll have supper there.

Her words shot out in a clatter. Her tone was odd. Almost excited.

I'll be back late, she said to Madeleine: I'll lock up when I come in.

She kissed them good night, quick smacks on the cheeks, one, two, they offered her.

Thérèse and Léonie were laying the table. Antoinette's place had to be laid opposite her husband's. He insisted. Her silver fork with the monogram engraved on the handle, her silver napkin ring. A form of remembrance. Madeleine called it ghoulish, but obeyed her brother-in-law's wishes. Now, hands on hips, she was checking the girls' work.

Don't forget Louis's pills, he has to take them with his food. And a bottle of wine, open one just in case he feels like a glass.

Victorine had on her beige raincoat, the green scarf, a woollen shawl, and her stout boots. As she left the dining-room her hand went to the bulge in her pocket. A lot of clothes just for crossing the farmyard on a warm autumn night. Not yet dark. They saw her plainly from the kitchen window when they ran to watch. Blue dusk began to blur shapes together, but the beige mackintosh was visible. Skipping past the poultry shed, excited, furtive. From their bedroom window they saw Victorine knock on Rose's door. The beige mackintosh was embraced by a blue one. Arm in arm they made off towards the kitchen-garden. Stealthy and eager as two crooks.

Supper was dismal. Like all the other meals nowadays. Louis sat listlessly in his place opposite his dead wife's high-backed chair and empty plate. He poked at his soup. The two girls were accustomed to not talking at meals. They clattered their spoons dutifully around their plates. Madeleine chattered to her brother-in-law. The weather, news of the farm, the village. He grunted. From time to time her voice trailed off and she became her grief, heavy as a stone. She carried it without complaining and without any comfort. She stared at her glass. Then she revived into cheering Louis.

Eat, she coaxed him: it'll do you good.

The two girls were swift as hares ushering the plates in and out. Louis's untasted food was scraped into the dogs' bowl, the baked leeks shut into the fridge, the cloth whisked off, shaken, folded away in the *buffet*. Thérèse flew at the washing-up while Léonie clattered coffee and *tisane* on to the silver tray and took it through into the white *salon*. Madeleine had on her spectacles and was reading the newspaper while Louis dozed on the sofa. She sighed as the two girls stood over her to kiss her good night.

Off to bed already? Sleep well then.

She no longer came in to kiss them once they were in bed. They were too old for that now. Teeth-cleaning, proper washing, saying of prayers, they were trusted to do those on their own. So their empty beds would not be noticed.

They copied Victorine and put on thick jumpers and raincoats and boots, just in case it was cold and wet in the woods. Léonie said that was where they were going. She just knew. Thérèse had the pocket torch she used for reading under the bedclothes. Léonie had a candle, candlestick, box of matches. She had a big bulge in her pocket, exactly like Victorine's.

They took their usual night-time route out of the house, via the backstairs and the dark kitchen. They glided out of the back door and leapt into a pit of shadow.

Tiptoe through the mud in the chilly dark. Crickets, owls, their own hasty breathing. No lights on in Rose's cottage. It thrust out at them, a black angle sharp as an elbow, as they went by. Stars overhead were frostily clear, Orion in front of them straddling the path.

In the furthest orchard they paused in front of the wall where the vine grew, and listened. Feet came along smartly over the sand and dirt of the path, were cushioned briefly by the grass of the bank into inaudibility, then snapped over twigs and beech-husks. Loud whispers, some giggles. From far inside the woods a thin music, a voice singing. Plaintive contralto. Victorine?

They pulled themselves to the top of the wall, sat there on the rough stone, shivering. Love made Léonie speechless. She thought: just suppose I saw her again. She did not dare say more. Love made her sharp-eyed too. She peered into the darkness of the lane. Thérèse beside her was calm and still.

People were coming from the village in groups of two and three, a stealthy procession. They knew their way all right. Steady and determined. Bulky shapes hatted and scarved against the cool night. Murmuring to each other, helping each other across the ditch then vanishing into the woods. In the close thickness of trees lights glimmered and swayed. Lanterns, Léonie thought: candles. She slipped from the wall down into the lane, pulled Thérèse after her. They were received by the group of villagers they joined with no comment other than a whispered *bonsoir*. Léonie recognized the blacksmith and his wife, their two teenage children. So they were all to be anonymous. Very well then. She crept forwards after them.

The little clearing in the heart of the woods looked different at night. Larger, its edges melted to blackness. Stars snapped overhead, through the branches. Thérèse and Léonie stood crushed up against adults they did not know. So many people here. Strangers, surely, from other farms, neighbouring villages. Damp wool and gaberdine in their nostrils, wide dark shoulders of men's coats looming above them, their noses pressed against foreign backs. Léonie loved it, this intimacy in the crowded dark. She was a spy, noting the spurt and lick of match-flame as someone lit a cigarette, the scent of rough tobacco, the light in the cupped hands, then the red tip of ash. Love made her reckless. She towed Thérèse through the pack of skirts and trouserlegs. They knocked against linked bodies, which parted to let them pass. Excuse me, excuse me. Now they were stumbling into the front row of people, on to rough grass. Now they were recognized, pushed forwards, blinking, to the glare of flames.

A bonfire blazed inside a small circle of stones. Tended by a woman with a long stick. She kept it tidy, the fire, pushing fallen embers into its heart, knocking its flaming hands together, greedy, bright. It was Rose. She nodded to them, went on with her stirring and poking.

Candles in jam-jars were set around the heap of boulders. Tongues of the holy spirit of the woods, that trembled but did not go out. Women knelt there, in the mud, among stones, candles clasped between their praying hands, their faces dramatically lit from underneath, their eyes turned towards the rock, the spring. A sigh shivered through them as Léonie and Thérèse joined them and knelt down.

Victorine was there too. She plucked the green scarf from the throat of her raincoat, spread it on top of the heap of boulders. She dressed her makeshift altar with a necklace of twisted corn, two jam-jars stuffed with bouquets of oats and barley.

Thérèse agitated her knees and rattled the rosary she'd produced from her pocket.

She whispered: she shouldn't be doing that.

Victorine gave a brisk nod, came to kneel down next to them. After a moment or two of uncertain waiting, someone started the rosary. Léonie was bored. She thought: she won't come, too many people.

Beside her Thérèse gasped. Became rigid. Her face tipped up, radiant. She opened her arms and smiled. The glow of the bonfire outlined her in gold.

That was the sign. Everyone, even the men, sank to their knees. All heads turned towards Thérèse, while the *Ave Maria* shot from their lips. Léonie closed her eyes and felt nothing.

Thérèse's ecstasy lasted through three decades of the rosary. Then, in the middle of a *Gloria*, she brought her outstretched hands back together, gave a funny little bow, and got stiffly to her feet. She seemed to know exactly what to do. She was poised, cheerful even. She lifted her hand, waved towards the crowd to get them standing up, and began the *Salve Regina*. Rose and Victorine stood one on each side of the heap of stones. Rose conducted, Victorine led the singing. They all knew the hymn. They sang it every week in church. *Mater misericordia*. A tune of much sweetness because so familiar.

But the tune changed halfway through. Now it leapt up and down, it gambolled. A man standing under the trees a little way off had produced an accordion and begun to play. The Latin words died, replaced by ones in *patois*.

People stretched, shook themselves, smiled. They looked at each other with a sudden lightheartedness that had gravity mixed into it. They bowed to each other like Thérèse had to the Virgin. Then they clasped hands and arms, began dancing. Léonie stood on a boulder to get a good view.

It was old-fashioned dancing. Like at the recent fête on the fifteenth of August, when rockets dashed upwards from the dark field outside the village and the Virgin ascended to heaven as a shower of fiery red sparks. Men and women dancing in formal couples, plenty of women together too. The sort of dancing where you hold your body straight and move from the knees. Much twinkling of booted feet, much strict twirling, heads held high, hands splayed in the small of backs, firm grips and spins. The accordion kept them at it, energetic, sweet. Here was Rose, she drew Léonie in.

Dancing was a consolation for not seeing the lady. At first they bumped each other, Rose's soft bosom a cushion for Léonie's chin. This made Léonie giggle; she rather liked it. But Rose was serious, hissing in her ear to behave properly, just concentrate. Between them they invented a sort of polka, in which their feet did not get too mixed up. They took turns at leading, each of them having begun by trying to be the man. Now they held each other in a practised and relaxed way, their heavy coats flying out behind them as they swept back and forth, back and forth. They wove in and out of other couples. The moon slid from the clouds and burned silver. A boy dangled a paper lantern over the dancers' heads, a globe of pleated paper with a lit candle inside, bobbing at the end of a pole, a second moon. It lurched in a sudden eddy of air, the dancers pushed on.

That dance stopped, and another began. Panting, delighted, Léonie leant against a tree, watching Rose trot, turn and swivel in the embrace of – was it? – yes, the postman. The secret party conferred adult status on her. She felt tall and languid, heated as though she had drunk wine. When a dark shape swam up at her and blotted the dancers from her view, she smiled, began to say yes of course I'll dance.

It was Baptiste. He clutched her against him too hard and too close. His breath warmed her ear, the side of her neck. He definitely did not believe in taking turns to be the man. He steered her in between the other villagers with fierce concentration. She thought oh well I'll let you, and her feet stopped insisting and darted in and out of his. She let herself press back against him. It was all right, because it was dark and they didn't have to talk. Two thicknesses of coat between them, she couldn't feel much. Rose and Victorine went past with a smile and a nod, feet severely in tune. Where was Thérèse? She had vanished. Léonie lifted her head from her partner's serge shoulder and stared about.

Baptiste apparently could read her mind.

She's gone home to bed, he growled in her ear: my mother says I'm to see you back.

Léonie was disappointed. And she had a sense of being got rid of. Though all about her the dancers were stopping, bowing and smiling, the atmosphere had heated up. The accordion had ceased. Bodies poised alertly. They expected. They knew what would happen next. And first, they waited for the outsiders to go, and for the sleepy children to slip off, melt away through the trees. The candles on the ground burned on.

Come on.

Baptiste took her hand and tugged her after him. Rose's face loomed suddenly, ecstatic and blank. She waved. She put her hand on Victorine's shoulder. Léonie couldn't watch them any more, she was being pulled on to the narrow track between the trees.

She knew the way back. Of course she did. Baptiste was making sure she didn't return to the clearing. No spying on adult secrets. At first she was blind in the dark, away from the candlelight, the soft glow of the bobbing lantern. Baptiste felt her stumble and slowed down so abruptly that she ran into him, grabbed at him to keep her balance.

Everyone had vanished. They were alone in the woods. Léonie's knees shook. Her stomach jumped up and down. Baptiste gripped her by the lapels, steered her off the path, shouldered her up against a tree. He stood over her and fumbled at her coat, opening it. His hands felt her rapidly. His mouth surrounded hers. Grazing it. She turned her head aside, met his cheek. He kissed her again. One hand on each side of her waist, he pinioned her, slid his tongue into her mouth. Warm and soft, he was in her. Léonie had one clear thought: he is pretending I am Thérèse. So she felt free to yield, enjoy herself: it's not me he's kissing, she explained to the nun in her head. His nose bobbed against hers. He worked his lips up and down, up and down, over hers. It seemed very businesslike. Soft, rubbery touches. Then his hands left her waist and burrowed under her jumper.

Baptiste stroked her tenderly, attentively. She thought of the drowning kittens and wanted to laugh. Both of them were breathing hard, such a hurry and scramble of lips, hands, such a heat inside and between them, he stuffed one small breast into his mouth and then the other, giving her the same churn of astonished guilty pleasure as when she lay on her bed in the afternoons and read the forbidden books she smuggled home from the library. Those books where so little, finally, was spelt out that Léonie's imagination took hold, she pressed down, down, on the pillows so carefully arranged underneath her, till the wave of warm sweetness toppled, fell, receded, and she lay back curled up eyes closed almost in pain. Those books Thérèse read too but pretended she didn't because then she'd have to go to confession about them and spell out exactly what she'd thought.

Now Léonie was thinking about Thérèse, how unfair it was boys wanted her when anyone could see, however well-developed her figure was, she wasn't interested in all that. In what Baptiste was doing now to her, Léonie whom he thought of as Thérèse, lifting her skirt, sliding his hand between her thighs, sliding his hand further up to touch her wet knickers. Léonie sighed. The nun in her head shouted out. That was as far as the books said you should go. Quite a lot farther. Stop *now*. She shook her head and sighed.

I want to go home. I'm going home now.

She walked in front of him. They climbed over the cold wall, into the orchard. Baptiste jerked his head at her, then disappeared into the darkness in the direction of Rose's cottage. Léonie picked her way up the kitchen-garden towards the house. Was that a light burning in one of the windows of the second floor? It flickered, then went out. Thérèse's room. Thérèse pretending to be asleep.

She stood outside the back door for a moment. Familiar smell, in the darkness, of salt-laden air, manure, compost. The strip of seaweed nailed by the door was slimy to her touch. A dog barked in one of the cottages. A car swished by on the main road. Everything was exactly as it always was. Léonie had just been kissed for the first time by a boy. More than just kissed, really. The sort of passionate encounter she had read about in novels. She had thought of that first male kiss as opening a door inside her, through which she would step towards adulthood, real sex. She expected to feel utterly changed. The possessor, at last, of secret knowledge. She lifted her feet, one by one, pressed them down on to the boot-scraper that stood by the back door. Lumps of mud fell off. She longed for a thick ham sandwich and her bed.

The kitchen door flew open. Madeleine looked out.

Where have you *been*?

Léonie was tempted to confess everything. To watch her mother go first pale with shock, then stiff with rage. To hear her stutter, then screech. You let a farm boy maul you about?! Probably there wouldn't be words sufficient to express the outrage. Léonie decided to reserve the pleasure of baiting Madeleine for later. She sounded as casual as possible.

I went for a walk in the woods. It was all right, there were lots of people there. Victorine. Rose and Baptiste.

Madeleine turned away.

I've been worried to death. I'm very disappointed in you.

THE WATER-BOTTLE

*L*éonie had agreed to help Victorine strip the tomato plants. Hauled from the corner where she was writing up her diary, she complained. Victorine insisted. Too much work and not enough people to do it. Where was Thérèse? That child always vanished just when you needed her.

On the way to the tomato patch they made a detour to Louis's workshop to collect some baskets. Big osier ones, flat, that you could crook over your arm or set on the ground. Her uncle sat at his workbench looking vague, as though he'd forgotten why he was there. His brown fingers played with one of the pieces of the broken Quimper dish. His eyes were watery, tears collected at the corners. Victorine pushed past him to collect the baskets.

She said: you should throw those bits away. That dish is unmendable. You're just wasting your time. Anyway there's a piece lost.

They made their stooping way up and down the rows of tomato plants. Two osier baskets each: one for red tomatoes and one for green. To save having to sort them later. With the green ones, every year, Louis made what he called frog jam. This year, Victorine snorted: she and Léonie would have to do it.

Why not chutney? Léonie enquired: like we do in England?

But she was too warm and lazy for a proper argument. The heat of the sun in this sheltered place made her not want to think about anything. She moved her hands among the leaves of the tomato plants, liking their roughness and hairiness, their harsh earthy smell, a bit sour, like that of geraniums. She liked breaking off the plump red fruits, each one crowned with a stalk like a star. Some were dusty and cracked, oozing juice they were so ripe. The green ones held on tighter, didn't plop into her palms but had to be tugged.

Here she is, said Victorine: here's *mademoiselle*.

Thérèse made her way through the neat kitchen-garden. She wore a striped blue and brown dress, dangled a net veil in one hand, clutched a bunch of red and purple gladioli in the other.

I'm going to put some flowers on Maman's grave, she said to Léonie: would you like to come?

Victorine measured the last two rows of unpicked tomatoes with her sharp blue eyes. She waved towards the baskets at her feet.

We've nearly finished. Go on, you might as well. Take these in for me first.

Léonie decided there was no time to put on a dress. But she stood in front of the large square mirror in the hall and lifted the gilt-backed brush she found there. She dabbed at her hair, smoothing it. She pulled her blouse down, found a cardigan.

The cemetery was a square plot of ground, enclosed by a high wall with ornamental turrets at the corners. The dead lay inside this fortified enclosure in rows as neat as those in the Martins' kitchen-garden. They rotted quietly, like the dropped fruit you found hidden under the leaves of the tomato plants. The older graves had crosses and stone angels, low wrought-iron fences. The modern ones were like fallen doors. Thick slabs of shiny granite. On top might be a porcelain book open at a bit of holy text, plus a photograph, or a porcelain cluster of pink and red roses with sharp frilled edges. Plastic pots of bright flowers were less ugly than the tombs, made the cemetery messy, even cheerful.

Here and there women tended the graves, just as they tended their houses. Swept and polished plots had their weeds removed, their flowers replaced, their carpets of blue and green marble chips pulled straight. One or two ancient graves were neglected, rusty iron crosses dangling broken beadwork bouquets. But most looked like dolls' houses, Léonie thought, where the women played at rearranging the clean furniture. Why did it matter so much where you were buried? That people knew, and came to visit you?

Thérèse knew that it mattered, but she did not say why. She was busy at the tap over in the far corner of the cemetery, filling the empty bottle she had brought with her from the house. Léonie stood by her aunt's grave, scuffing her sandal in the dust of the path and reciting the Hail Mary under her breath because she felt she should. Antoinette lay in the earth, crushed by a smooth black slab. Incised letters, filled in with gold, spelt out her name and dates. Like the cover of a book. Which was supposed to open and flap back at the end of the world and let her out, resurrected. Léonie looked around. A garden of books, each with its title and date. Characters staggering out from between the pages on the Day of Judgment, brushing earth from their lips. People in books did not die.

She chanted aloud: now and at the hour of our death amen.

Thérèse returned with her water-bottle, knelt down to arrange her flowers. Gladioli blazing out of their thick green sheaths, sprigs of speckled green and yellow laurel. She crossed herself, closed her eyes. Her expression became dreamy, ecstatic. Léonie looked away and coughed.

They walked out through the wrought-iron gates. Léonie dragged these to behind her.

She said: I'm going to go to the woods again tonight. Will you come too? I want to see more of what's going on.

Thérèse upended the empty bottle she carried, shaking it. A couple of drops flew out.

I don't know, she said: I don't think I want to. I didn't like it when it turned into a dance. I couldn't find you so I went home.

Oh, Léonie said: I was dancing with Baptiste.

Were you! Thérèse said.

She marched ahead, very fast, her back straight, the bottle grasped by the neck, like a club. Léonie caught her up, tapped her shoulder.

Eh, eh, calm down will you.

She tweaked Thérèse's earlobe: slow down!

Thérèse shook her off: let go of me!

Léonie wheeled. Instead of following Thérèse down the road that led to the centre of the village, out again, and so, eventually, to the Martin farm, she went in the other direction. The long way round. The path through the fields, that ran past the back of the farm, and the woods. She refused to look round, even though she was sure that the angry Thérèse, determined to miss nothing, was behind her. She counted the telegraph poles, cows behind the electric fence, her own heartbeats. This was one of Thérèse's record silences if you didn't include the ones during her illness.

Thérèse drew level with her.

The thing is, Léonie, it's rather vulgar, isn't it? There's Our Lady appeared to us and you let yourself be pawed by some boy from the farm. It's not really on you know.

You weren't really asleep when I came in last night, were you? Léonie said: you were just pretending. And you told Maman that I was out in the woods.

She peeped sideways at Thérèse's breasts, hips, calves. Never mind, Madeleine always said to the flinching Thérèse: wide hips are best for having babies. And to Léonie: never mind, you'll see when you grow up, it's fashionable to be thin.

They reached the back of the Martin property, the orchard wall.

Anyhow it's you he fancies, Léonie announced.

Thérèse was pink as a boiled prawn.

I don't care! she shouted.

She jumped across the ditch that marked the entrance to the woods. She turned back towards Léonie, with a recomposed face.

We've come to say our prayers to Our Lady, haven't we? To see whether she'll appear again? So let's be like we are in church, all right?

The wood was full of noises. Crashes in the undergrowth. The whine of psalms as squeezed out of the village choirboys. The tinkling of a gold bell. Loud Latin words in a clerical voice. Léonie sniffed at a current of incense that drifted past, cold and pungent. It smelled all wrong in these woods.

Rose barred their way. She seemed to have jumped up from nowhere. Out of a bush. She raised her finger at them.

It's *Monsieur le Curé*. Don't let him see you. It'll only mean trouble.

She spoke in a whisper. Thérèse whispered back.

But what's he doing? That's Our Lady's shrine. Is he saying Mass?

No, Rose said: he's been doing an exorcism. He says the apparitions are the work of the Devil. He's been casting the Devil out.

She put her hand on Thérèse's arm.

Don't go and look. You'll only get upset.

The girls ran past her, into the clearing. Word of the priest's intentions must have spread very fast, for many of the villagers were there, shop workers and farm labourers all mixed up, just like last night. In church they kept to their own groups, but here they jostled shoulder to shoulder, watchful and sulky. Last night's jam-jars, with their stubs of candle, had been knocked over. The posies of corn had been trampled in the mud. Victorine's green scarf, torn almost in two, flapped from a nearby branch.

The wobbly singing of the little choir stopped. One of the altar-boys looked about uncertainly, then went on swinging his censer. Another struggled to relight his taper, extinguished by the wind. A third held a bucket of holy water towards the priest. *Monsieur le Curé* controlled his wind-whipped surplice, stole and skirts with one angry hand. With the other he dipped what looked like a hearthbrush into the bucket then flung its load of holy-water drops all over the pile of stones. He glared, and crossed himself. Loudly he intoned some short Latin prayer, then crossed himself again and turned. He came across the clearing followed by his retinue.

The people drew back to let him pass. They bent their heads and turned away, muttering in *patois*. Only Thérèse stood fast, shoulders back and chin up. She barred his way. Léonie beside her wanted to run away from this red-faced furious man. Thérèse dropped to her knees and tried to kiss his ring. He jerked his hand away. You only kissed bishops' rings, even Léonie knew that, Thérèse must have forgotten.

The priest shouted, so that everyone could hear.

I've given my orders. By tomorrow night that pile of stones will have been pulled down and this pagan nonsense completely done away with.

He stared at Thérèse.

As for you, you'd better come to see me this afternoon. Tell your father to come with you, I want a word with him too.

He was off in a swirl of lace and black skirts. Léonie felt very relieved. She didn't have to go too and be grilled. The priest didn't know about the golden-red lady. She was safe. She ran across the clearing and tugged down Victorine's scarf from the tree.

THE ROSARY

M onsieur *le Curé* kept himself shut away from his parishioners in a large stone house. A long thin garden of lawn and ornamental cypresses, enclosed by shrubs and then by iron railings, separated it from the boulevard between the cemetery and the church.

People were not encouraged to call at his house. None of the Martins, as far as Thérèse knew, had ever been inside it. The priest was left in peace outside his sorties forth to say Mass and hear confessions and have lunch with what Madeleine, waving her cigarette, called *the better families*. He hadn't been to the Martins' for lunch since Antoinette died. A relief to Léonie, not to have to observe him sitting knees crossed in the best armchair daintily sipping his *apéritif*, one hand going up to smooth his shining black hair. In between courses he would wash his hands in the air and speak with a pulpit authority laced with a show of charm. It was hard to decide whether she loathed him more inside church or out.

You can't imagine him going into one of the labourers' cottages can you, Thérèse said, pulling on her nylons.

Nor having a shit, said Léonie: nor lying in bed. What kind of pyjamas does he wear I wonder? Purple and gold bri-nylon, with a dog-collar. While you're there you'll be able to find out. And he won't dare be too rude to you because you're not a peasant. Not like Saint Bernadette.

Thérèse looked noble for a minute, like one of her favourite virgin martyrs about to be broken on the wheel. Then she relapsed into gloom. Léonie picked up the brush and got going on her cousin's hair.

Just don't let him bully you that's all.

There was a truce between them at the moment. The priest had done it with orders for the pile of stones to be pulled down. Léonie smiled at Thérèse in the mirror and zipped her up at the back. She fastened the clasp of the gold crucifix Thérèse always wore now on a thin gold chain around her neck. Antoinette had left it to her, plus some gold bangles and a string of pearls. To Léonie she left an ivory bracelet and a silver brooch.

Thérèse, poured into a tube of blue linen, sighed. She got up, picked up her white gloves, her shoulder-bag of blue quilted plastic with a gilt chain. Shoulders back at the angle recommended by *L'Echo de la mode*, chin up, stomach sucked in. On her high heels she teetered downstairs to join her father.

Louis had put on his grey suit, and carried his beret. Thérèse sprang at him, kissed him on both cheeks. They went out to the car. Léonie watched them from her window upstairs, her hand wound in the muslin curtain.

Monsieur le Curé's house, pinkish-grey stone faced with white, was dark inside. The housekeeper showed them into an antechamber bleak as a dentist's waiting-room. The mottled tiles of the floor were slimy purple like uncooked liver. Curtains of closely woven cotton lace were stretched across the windows, fastened so tightly they kept out both air and sun. A single aspidistra gleamed in one corner in a lime-green ceramic pot. The walls were papered dim brown. Christ writhed on a knobbly wooden crucifix next to a photograph of the Pope. A pleated white paper fan perched in the empty grate below.

The room smelled of winter and of washing. Thérèse imagined the housekeeper wiping the aspidistra with a soapy sponge, rinsing down the ivory Christ, loincloth and all, holding him in her arms like a baby with a wet nappy. *Monsieur le Curé* sat in his bath, a huge holy-water stoup, still holding his biretta, while the housekeeper washed his bristly black hair. These were thoughts sent by the Devil. She shut her eyes and prayed furiously for deliverance.

She opened them to find that the priest had come in and was blandly regarding her and her father. She did the bob they were taught at school, the deep version. The two men sat down in red velvet chairs on opposite sides of the cold fireplace, glared at by Christ and the Pope. Thérèse stood between them, hands clasped. Her shoes began to pinch her toes, like a warning to run away, and she was suddenly desperate to go to the lavatory. More distractions from the Devil.

Monsieur le Curé moved his long fingers, which he clearly admired, over the skirts of his black soutane. He sounded, when he spoke, as deliberately bored as possible.

Well then, my dear friend, so what's all this gossip in the village about visions of Our Blessed Lady? I must say I'd have thought I could rely on you to calm people down.

Louis spoke, letting go of his beret to spread his hands. The black armband strained on one sleeve. He was humble, he shrugged, he mentioned that Thérèse was a truthful child.

The priest listened, head on one side. His confession pose. The heron profile that she saw through the grille. She hadn't been to confession since the vision. Couldn't. His fingers were clasped now, supporting his chin. The most delicate of yawns. His voice, when finally he deigned to open his mouth, was smooth. Thérèse jumped. The cool grey eyes swerved, rested on her.

Farradiddle. Yes my girl that's what I said. I've never heard of such nonsense.

Thérèse dared to interrupt his strictures when he paused for breath.

But Father I did see her. And she told me her name when I asked, she said Mary Mother of God.

The priest looked at her with contempt.

What do you suppose you are, some sort of little saint?

He went on, more to her father now than to her, in his light drawling voice she had to listen to in church every Sunday of her life telling them all what was what because he had the God-given power to do so and they had to listen and obey. That was what being a Catholic meant. Thérèse tried to remember that the priest represented Christ and must be right. The blood rushed to her cheeks, swelled and thickened them. Her chin wobbled, she couldn't control it, however hard she tried not to cry as his words reached her. Young girls of a certain age. Impressionable, heated imaginations, hysteria. Romanticize. Idealistic. Thérèse stared at her black patent shoes, those twin vices crushing her toes, telling her to take her feet away. She tried to concentrate on that particular pain. She gritted her teeth. She wiped her wet palms on the back of her dress. Between her thighs, stuck together, moisture slipped.

The priest glanced at her and threw up his hands.

Oh no, no tears, I beg of you. You see? You're just an ordinary little girl. A true visionary wouldn't crumple at the first sign of opposition, would take all this in her stride.

He turned back to Louis, who sat calm and polite in his chair, who didn't turn to look at Thérèse. The thread that bound them had snapped with one expert tug. The priest's tone grew stern.

What convinces me that this child is deluded is the conflicting reports of the so-called apparition. Some say she is robed in blue, others in yellow and red. Red, I ask you! Some say she has long fair hair, others that she's as dusky a beauty as you'd find among the *pieds-noirs*!

Thérèse interrupted him.

No, that's not true, Father. It's Our Lady, dressed in blue. She's got long fair hair but she's got a veil over it.

She lowered her eyes to avoid the priest's glance. He laughed and went on, addressing Louis again.

All this is extremely bad for your daughter's reputation my dear friend. She's making herself a laughing-stock. Dangerous pagan nonsense. Idiotic outdated folklore. In these days of religious renewal. Low sort of gossip. Pernicious tales put about by the likes of Rose Taillé and her layabout son.

Thérèse's tears splashed on to the tiles at her feet. The priest looked pleased at her collapse. He tapped her on the shoulder. She felt his fingers spring away again, relieved. He picked up a rosary of cheap light beads that lay coiled in an alabaster ashtray on a side table near the door.

Here, child. Take this with you, it's been blessed by the Holy Father and it will do you good to use it. Say a decade of the rosary next time you're tempted to imagine you're seeing visions and the Devil won't be able to harm you. On your knees for half an hour every night with your rosary, that's the right thing for young girls chasing holiness. One last thing: I forbid you to go to the woods again.

They were dismissed. Bladder clenched, Thérèse limped down the drive behind her silent father.

Next day, Sunday, she sat between him and Léonie in church. She still had not been to confession. She decided not to go to communion. Suppose, suppose, she were in a state of mortal sin? Or that the priest refused her?

The stone interior of the church held darkness as a curved shell holds water. The statues of the saints were ranged along the walls in clumps of two and three, like groups of chatty friends. God hid in the domed box on the altar. Don't abandon me, Thérèse silently begged: don't.

The priest ascended the steps to the pulpit. Below him, the altar-boys settled on their bench, hands in their sleeves, as scornful as he who drilled them week after week. Wrapped in lace and linen, they stared at the women and girls forbidden to enter the sanctuary.

The theme of the sermon was reverence and obedience. Waywardness of certain elements of the youth in the parish. Authority of our Holy Mother the Church vested in me. Regular attendance at Mass and the sacraments, especially confession, as ordained by Holy Church. The sheep guided by the shepherd. Undesirable elements of individualism and mysticism, undesirable attempts at originality, to be weeded out. Adolescent frailty and need of guidance. Saint Paul and Saint Augustine on women.

Thérèse sweated with shame. She stared at her lap where her hands, gloved in tight white net, gripped her missal. She pressed her knees together. If she pressed very hard then her mouth would not open to scream. Torrents of lava would not tumble out to force fire down his throat, torch his tongue. She was red and liquid and dangerous. She would damage that priestly flesh, oh yes, scorch it, she would tear his head very slowly from his neck and laugh as the blood gushed. She would shut him up, trample him down, stop up his mouth for ever with hot red mud.

She couldn't hear him any longer. White peace descended and surrounded her like a tent of cool white gauze. God was in the tent. God was the tent. He surrounded her and wrapped her up in the folds of his silence, his mystery. His great heartbeat near hers. She lay on his heart and did nothing. She let go of her hot grief, which dissolved and became the dew on his garments. He was the coolness at the centre of the fire and his look purged and freed her. She was with him, unafraid. She was nothing and she was love and she was a voice singing in the desert, full of trust, full of gladness at her deliverance.

Beside her Léonie shifted from one buttock to the other and coughed loudly. The priest glared at her then swept on with his discourse. Thérèse didn't hear him. She didn't feel Léonie's elbow jab hers. She was rapt in a frame of fiery clouds. She no longer spoke to anyone except God. She chose silence, obscurity, poverty. She chose him who was everything, her hollow in the rock, her desert refuge. She rose to meet her future self. She flew towards it.

Thérèse's faint in the middle of the priest's sermon spoilt its effect. Though he continued his tirade, people were distracted. They craned their necks to watch the white-faced girl, limp as a corpse, carried out in her father's arms.

It was a sign, but of what kind? Was it the Virgin rescuing her own or the Devil showing he was beaten? Had Thérèse had a fit? Was she indeed making it all up? The little knots of people that formed as usual outside the church after Mass was over and the bells were tumbling out their soft dismissal song had plenty to discuss. Léonie stood amongst them, next to Madeleine and Rose. Victorine was the one who brought the news. The men destroying the heap of stones in the woods, on the orders of the priest, had found that it covered a shallow grave. Inside this was a mess of human skulls and bones.

THE CAKE TIN

Madeleine was seated at the little writing-desk in the back corridor on the first floor. From time to time she sighed. She was checking a column of figures, Léonie could see. She hovered, peering over her mother's shoulder to see how she was getting on. Madeleine started adding up again, nodding her head as her eyes strayed down the page, moving her lips. This time she was satisfied. She ticked the sum and underlined the total. It was a bill sent by the village undertaker. *Pompes Funèbres* in queer modern lettering, thick and black. She sighed again.

Léonie galloped in with her question. *The* question.

But whose bones *were* they?

Madeleine tucked a curl behind her ear. She lit a cigarette, sucked expertly. Her words drifted like smoke.

Oh. From the war.

But why bury them there? Léonie persisted: why not in the cemetery?

Men from the village had fought in two world wars. The names of those who had died in battle were inscribed on a stone roll of honour on the war memorial by the cemetery. Every village had one. Blémont's was a heartily built stone woman in clinging robes carrying a wreath and a scroll. Her hair tumbled loose, her breasts were pointed. She wasn't Our Lady, Madeleine had explained to the children years ago: she was *La France*, also *La République*. It was on Our Lady's feast-day, though, that the village remembered its dead. On the fifteenth of August, after High Mass. The village band, all discordant trumpetings and squeaks, led the congregation in procession to the war memorial. The national anthem was played. Everyone bowed their heads. Later on that day there would be the fair, fireworks, and dancing, but now they were still, quiet. Baptiste played in the band. He wore a brown uniform and carried a cornet in shining yellow brass. Our Lady ascended to heaven on the fifteenth of August and looked after *La République*. When you were in France you were certain Our Lady was French. You felt that she passionately cared about the French soldiers and made sure they won the war. You felt, like Victorine, that the French were the best.

Madeleine said: they couldn't be buried in the cemetery if people had forgotten all about them and didn't know where they were, could they?

But why had people forgotten? Léonie asked.

Timidly she tacked on another question that bothered her.

Why didn't any women die in the war?

Madeleine put down her pen and knocked her cigarette ash into a blue Limoges dish like a saucer.

Look. You and your questions can't you see I'm busy?

Léonie waited. She could see there was more to come.

Madeleine said in a rush: one more thing. You're not to go to the woods any more. I absolutely forbid it. You'll only get yourself into trouble. You don't understand what these people are like. I don't want you mixing with children like Baptiste. You know I've always believed that people from different back-grounds shouldn't mix, it's not fair on the children. You're much too young to be thinking about boys, when I was your age I went around in a big friendly group, plenty of time for all that later on.

Léonie wandered downstairs. She imagined the children of mixed marriages: striped black and white, like badgers. In the kitchen she found Victorine tightly absorbed in skimming the thick skin off the saucepan of milk she had just boiled. She cocked an eye at Léonie, grunted.

I'm going to make *gâteau à la peau de lait* for supper. You can help if you want.

It was a cake you never got in England, because there the milk did not have to be boiled and so you could never collect a bowlful of creamy skin from successive goes. Victorine opened the fridge door and took out a fluted blue bowl clotted with white. She measured the amount with one quick look.

Yes. Just enough.

The cake was everyone's favourite. A sort of sponge, low and crusty and golden, which they ate with apricot jam. Léonie tied on an apron and hoisted herself on to a kitchen chair.

She asked: but whose bones *were* they?

Victorine steadily beat the cream in the bowl. Léonie sifted silky flour on to the wide brass pan of the scales.

Well, Victorine said at last: possibly Jews. And possibly someone who was trying to help them. Escape from the Germans I mean. They got caught and so they were shot.

Léonie plucked out the brass weights from their deep plush-lined nests in the wooden box. They fitted into these exactly. She grasped each one by its golden nipple and set it on the scales. She liked the way they were graded in the box by size, tiny to large. Like children herded into line for a family snap. She used a combination of small weights, to have the fun of adding them up.

She remarked: but in the war the Germans were fighting the French. Jews aren't French, they're Jews.

Victorine tipped flour into cream and beat again.

A lot of the Jews were French citizens. The point was the Germans hated them and wanted to get rid of them. Surely you know that. Don't they teach you anything in English schools?

Léonie said: the war's too modern for us to do it in history. We're doing the Tudors and Stuarts.

She watched Victorine grease the cake tin. Rapid strokes of a pastry brush dipped into golden oil.

She said: but why did the Germans hate the Jews?

Victorine balanced the cake tin on the palm of her outstretched hand and frowned at it.

A lot of people did in those days. Things were different then.

Even French people? Léonie asked.

Some French people. Yes.

Did you? Léonie persisted.

Victorine slapped the cake tin down on to the table and poured cake mixture into it, helping the thick flow along with a rubber spatula. Her voice was a shrug.

Of course not. As long as they weren't making trouble and thinking they were better than us.

She pushed the empty bowl across the table towards Léonie.

Here. Lick it if you like. But shut up for a bit will you, I've got to get on.

Léonie hesitated. She was a bit too old for licking bowls, wasn't she? She tapped her forefinger on the bowl's edge.

But why weren't they buried in the cemetery after they were shot?

Victorine clattered the cake into the oven.

The Germans took them away in secret, at night. Then in the early morning, just before dawn, they took them into the woods and shot them. They buried the bodies themselves. Nobody knew where. The grave was never found.

Léonie asked: but how do you know?

Victorine shouted: I'm busy, be quiet will you?

THE PACKAGE

The postbox was made of white wood. It hung on the outside of the small wrought-iron gate set in the brick wall at the main entrance. People and cars always came in through the big double gates. The small one was wreathed in weeds and brambles no one bothered to clear away. Even though it meant that going to fetch the letters gave you scratches and nettle-stings. Madeleine kept repeating that she'd get down to hacking back the brambles one of these days but on the other hand she didn't have the time. The girls did not volunteer for the job. Thérèse because she was indifferent to the acid jab of nettles, Léonie because she liked to see that little corner of the grounds turned untidy and wild, the gateposts swarming with weeds and grass in their crevices, clumps of Michaelmas daisies.

The postman usually bicycled up around mid-morning, a time when everyone in the house was busy or pretending to be. They rarely noticed him arrive. By the time Madeleine remembered to go and check the box it was nearly lunch-time and she was making *hors d'œuvres* with one hand and pouring *apéritifs* with the other. In the days just after Antoinette's funeral, however, the postman brought bundles of letters to the kitchen door. Too many to cram down the slit of the little wooden box. He brought village news, too, titbits that Victorine indicated she had already gleaned in her trips to the shops. He would float these across the kitchen to her while implacably she checked the meat roasting in the oven for lunch. Oh yes? she'd say, polite and distant: oh really? And she'd nod meaningfully in the direction of the hovering Léonie: not in front of the children please. All Léonie managed to discover from the postman's hints was that the priest had had the bones taken away for a quick burial in the cemetery with as few people present as possible, and that people were still visiting the site of the apparitions, waiting to see whether Thérèse would go back.

Léonie had her first period on the day that Madeleine finished replying to all the letters of condolence sent to Louis. He wasn't expected by her or Victorine to reply to them, Léonie saw. He wrote business letters and that was it. Madeleine stuck on a final stamp then took Léonie upstairs. She kitted her out in a belt and a thick wad of gauze. This felt soft, rather comfortable, a bulky caress between the legs. Léonie held herself straight so that no one should know her secret. She felt different but didn't know how to express it. Not walking wounded. Not more grown-up. It was like putting on a costume for a play, or running in the three-legged race. Madeleine gave her a quick kiss, then tossed her the postbox keys.

All right darling? Go and check for letters will you? I must see if Louis is all right. It'll do you good to get a breath of air. You look a bit pale.

Léonie collected Thérèse and they went across the white gravel in the sunshine. Léonie strutted stiff-legged like a cowboy. She felt wetness leave her and sink into the towel. Thérèse didn't seem to have noticed. Léonie wondered if she were extremely pale or just moderately so. It was the kind of thing Antoinette would have commented on. Now Madeleine had taken over doing that. Her stomach clenched itself and ached. Between her legs the wetness gushed again.

Thérèse insisted it was her right, as the daughter of the house, to fit the little black iron key into the lock and turn it. Léonie lifted up the wooden flap and peered into what always seemed to her like a bird-house in which they might find golden eggs. Two letters for Louis. Cheap envelopes of rough paper, one blue, one greeny-grey. The colour of thrushes' eggs. No trace of magical peacocks. No phoenixes rising reborn from the raging red fire. A Catholic newsletter addressed to Antoinette, *L'Echo de la mode* for Madeleine, and some sort of bill in a white envelope with a pearly paper window.

Léonie had hardly written to her schoolfriends in England that summer. She did not know how to describe her life in France, had never done so. It required a language that her English friends did not share. Froggy, they put on their postcards to her, rocked with laughter at the thought of her eating horse steaks and snails. Now that she was going to stay on in France for a while and not go back to her old school, she'd already let go of those friends. They didn't matter. They faded out, a blur of English sounds, hearty, absurd, foreign. Still she wished someone had written to her. She wished she had a letter. She scowled at her sandals and scuffed them on the gravel. With Thérèse at her side she began to walk back towards the house.

A shout made them look up. The postman was pedalling back towards them down the road. He drew up on the other side of the tall white gates and fished in his grey sack.

Sorry, he called: I forgot this one.

He held a package in his hands. He raised it, threw it over the small postbox gate. It dropped into Thérèse's hands. He waved, and bicycled off again.

The parcel was substantial, tightly wrapped in brown paper, crisscrossed by waxed brown twine with many knots. One white label stuck on the front and one on the back.

It's for me, Thérèse exclaimed: it's from the nuns in Sœur Dosithée's old convent.

She opened it upstairs, in her bedroom, where no one except Léonie would see. She wanted a secret. Also to examine one. She cut through the tight bonds of twine, the shiny brown wrappings, with Léonie's penknife. A crust of brown corrugated paper required the knife again. Like slicing into pastry, Léonie thought: to see what kind of pie you'd got. Four and twenty blackbirds. Or magpies. Four and twenty black and white nuns singing the praises of God baked in a pie.

Thérèse lifted out bunches of letters held together by rubber bands. All of them, she saw as she flicked through them, addressed to Sœur Dosithée, and all of them signed *your loving sister Antoinette*. Blue, white, cream, grey envelopes, that had been neatly slit open. A calm nun's hand wielding a paper-knife. Self-control: waiting until the hour of recreation, when letters from home were allowed to be read. Not so would Léonie treat a letter. If someone sent me one, she thought: I'd tear it open straight away, I couldn't wait.

The gong for lunch sounded two floors down.

But why did they send them to you? Léonie said: and not to Madeleine. It must be a mistake.

It says Mademoiselle Martin, Thérèse said: and that's me. It's quite right I should have them. They must have realized how I'd cherish them. What use would your mother have for them? She'd probably throw them away. She only likes modern things.

She collected up the letters and stuffed them back, higgledy-piggledy, into their brown paper and cardboard nest.

I won't read them just yet. First I'll find them a good hiding-place.

They ran downstairs together. On the first landing Thérèse uttered a shriek when Léonie overtook her.

Do something. Quick. Don't let them see. You've got a huge red stain all down the back of your shorts.

Thérèse found Léonie a fresh towel. The pad like a hammock, Léonie thought, held in its net of gauze. She lowered herself on to it, snug.

You should wear a skirt, Thérèse explained: so that no one can see. Otherwise you might have a bulge showing.

She showed Léonie how to roll up the used towel in a paper bag, smuggle it down the backstairs into the kitchen, bury it in the red heart of the range. They walked into the dining-room together only five minutes late. Clean white half-moons of nails held out for inspection, hands reddened from hot water and soap, hair brushed. Proper *jeunes filles*. Which meant having secrets.

THE IRONING-BOARD

On Mondays the wash was hung out to dry on the clothes-lines at the end of the kitchen-garden nearest to the house. By mid-afternoon the first batch was almost dry, still slightly damp, just right for ironing, and could be fetched in by Victorine and whichever child she could catch to help her. It took two people quite a time to take the big sheets down one by one, flap and fold them, holding the corners tight. Then you had to unpeg all the other linen and clean clothes and cart it all upstairs to the *lingerie* in round two-handled baskets.

Rose had gone on coming in to help Victorine. She came when it suited her, when she could spare the time from her other work, but she always popped in on Monday afternoons to make a start on the ironing.

Is Rose coming today? Léonie asked: she missed last Monday.

She and Victorine held on to a great square sheet. As they tugged it straight the wind bellied it out, taut as a sail.

She was at the funeral, Victorine said: she would go, poor thing. She'll be along soon. She told me she'd come today.

I'll help you, shall I? Léonie said to Rose: I'd like to give you a hand.

Rose was wearing a dull black cardigan over a black dress. Although she was a widow, she didn't usually wear black. She wore blue checks, or brown. For gardening she wore a scarlet jumper. Today her nose and cheeks showed red under the powder, and her one good eye was red-rimmed, as though she'd been crying. Her green glass eye didn't care. It shone as usual. She joked with Victorine in the kitchen as quick as ever, then drank the last of her cup of coffee and got up.

All right then, she said to Léonie: if you want to.

They lugged the baskets of laundry upstairs together to the *lingerie*. It was at the far end of the attics. A small room. A box for linen. In the centre was the ironing-board made out of an old table covered with a blanket and a sheet. These were marked with brown triangles. Traces of an overheated iron allowed to pause face-down. Shirts and sheets they hung from the ceiling, draping them on lines and hangers. Damp, fragrant veils that made a cool tent around the central space of heat where Rose began to ply the heavy iron. The hot smell of ironing mixed with that of garden-dried linen. Added in was Rose's own smell, warm animal washed with lily-of-the-valley soap. Fresh air and sweat and scorched cloth: that was the smell of their conversation.

Rose, as she listened to Léonie's questions, took off her black cardigan, rolled up her black sleeves. Her face, as she worked and talked, reddened, till she was as rosy as her name.

The Germans were highly organized, she said, pushing the blue-and-white enamelled iron back and forth: they hunted up all the Jews they could find. Regular round-ups. The really big one in Paris, we called it *la grande rafle*.

She finished the collar, began on a sleeve. The cuff first. Dancing the iron over its crisp edge.

They kept the Jews in a sports stadium outside Paris. Packed in with hardly any food or water. Of course lots of them died. Then they were sent to the camp at Drancy, and from there they were put on trains and sent to Auschwitz to be gassed.

To send, Léonie thought: letters, packets. How did you send people in their thousands from one side of Europe to another? She concentrated on this problem so that she did not have to imagine the people themselves. Sent off to become parcels of ash.

Freight trains, Rose said: people jammed in standing up, into trucks. Without food or water. For a journey that took three days. Afterwards, we found out. Those who wanted to know that is.

The sleeve was too dry. She banged the iron down on to its tin rest, took up a small bowl of water, sprinkled the sleeve. The spots of damp hissed under her iron.

Anyway, some Jews did manage to escape the round-ups. One family from Rouen, a couple with their young daughter, turned up here in the village. Henri and I sheltered them for a while, but of course it was very risky with the Germans billeted everywhere except the smallest cottages.

She finished the second sleeve, began on the front. She frowned in concentration but at the same time she suddenly looked very tired, as though she should stop and sit down. The arm moving the iron dragged itself forward and back.

Somebody from the village must have betrayed us, because the Germans came in the night and took the Jewish family away. They took Henri as well. In the morning, just before it was light, they took them into the woods and shot them. They hid the grave so that we couldn't give the bodies a proper burial. They must have guessed we wouldn't look under the shrine. We'd all kept away from it ever since the priest had had it pulled down the month before. We never thought they'd dare put the bodies there.

Rose's voice was so dry that Léonie kept quiet. She watched the nose of the iron poke between the pearl buttons on Louis's shirt, thick cotton of silvery blue with a faint red stripe. Every time afterwards when she saw her uncle wear that shirt she remembered the words that Rose spoke.

None of us knew for certain who the informer was. Some people swore it must have been someone in the Martin family. Others said it must have been that girl who worked here, the one who was the German officer's mistress, she knew everything that was going on around here. Well, we all did. No one ever found out who it was. And then once the war was over people wanted to forget. But I can't.

Rose whipped the sleeves of the shirt behind its back, folded them like double-jointed elbows, bent the shirt in two, and gave it a final press on top.

I was expecting a baby at the time. I went into labour early. The baby was born dead.

THE ONYX ASHTRAY

They all assumed that Louis's stroke was the result of his grief. His wife, his strong prop, pulled away, and he leaned on air. Victorine said he had run down, like a watch. He had broken.

The girls were allowed to visit him in the clinic. They tiptoed along corridors shining and antiseptic, peeped at him where he lay, inert, in his white bed. He could not speak to them, though his mouth tried to. His lips worked, strained, around his lolling tongue. Something in his face fought, clawed, was smothered. Tears slid down his cheeks. Thérèse cried too, and had to go out. The nurse in charge, as coldly white as the bed and the room, said they were too noisy. They disturbed the other patients and should not come again. All the way home in the car Thérèse wept for her father. Léonie edged away from her on the warm plastic seat. Her thighs itched, encased in scratchy bronze nylons. She closed her eyes, tried to summon the image that consoled. But the golden-red lady did not come. Léonie could not remember her face. It dissolved into a black blindfold, a black gag.

The priest came to condole with Madeleine. Thérèse had to offer him the *apéritif*, Léonie the fluted glass dish of polished Japanese crackers. When Madeleine offered him a cigarette, he hesitated, then took one. Thérèse glanced away in disdain. No wonder enclosed nuns had to pray night and day for priests when they were so worldly.

Madeleine pushed a green onyx ashtray within his reach.

You'll have to forgive me, Father, but I can't repress my curiosity.

Her way of leaning forwards, eyes sparkling, fingers almost touching the priest's black sleeve, made Thérèse squirm. Really, women should not assume such familiar manners with priests. It suggested they did not sufficiently respect the vow of celibacy. It made them temptresses. It wasn't fair on the priests.

Madeleine said: what's going to happen with the shrine in the woods? Do tell us. We're all so longing to know.

Well, Thérèse supposed: Madeleine was a widow. She lacked male company. She'd no hope of remarrying if she stayed here, there was no one suitable in the village. Women of that age, she'd read somewhere, often made a push for one final fling. Madeleine was too old, though, to be behaving so girlishly. And her skirt was too short. When she crossed her legs you could almost see her stocking-tops. Luckily the priest had very good manners. He appeared not to notice his hostess's flirtatious twinkle. There was even a certain warmth when he glanced at Thérèse, as though he understood how embarrassed she was by her aunt's lack of dignity. She'd been living in England such a long time, of course, it was a bit too free and easy over there.

He said: the Bishop is coming down tomorrow to see me. I feel that some sort of ceremony of blessing of the place may be in order, now that the remains have been given a proper burial, and I have asked for his opinion. In all things I desire to be ruled by Our Holy Mother the Church.

He glanced severely at the two girls.

Won't you allow the shrine to be rebuilt? Madeleine asked: wouldn't that be a good thing for everyone?

He hesitated.

Some sort of stone memorial, at the place where they fell, to heroes who gave their lives for France, yes, the Bishop thinks that may be in order.

He crushed out his cigarette.

And how is my dear friend Monsieur Martin?

Good news, Madeleine said: he's coming home tomorrow. It was only a slight stroke, after all. But he can't talk yet.

He can't talk? the priest murmured: how very distressing.

He took his leave. Madeleine grimaced after she'd shut the door on him. Two small whiskies and her words were unguarded.

It looks better, doesn't it, if he agrees with what the Bishop wants. When of course you can see he wants the whole thing hushed up.

Why? asked Léonie.

Madeleine was instantly vague.

Oh. I don't know. I must go and see what Victorine's up to.

THE FISH-KETTLE

*T*he ambulance was expected at midday. Thérèse scooted through breakfast to give herself time for everything she had to do. Get Louis's room ready. Prepare lunch. Put on her best frock. Hastily she swallowed her coffee and bread, wiped the crumbs from her mouth and got up.

Hearing noises in the little white *salon* as she passed its door, she poked her head in to see what was going on. A bed had been put in one corner. Madeleine was whipping a stiff white sheet on to it, mitring the corners, folding back the top edge with its embroidered monogram.

Why are you moving him down here? Thérèse cried: I was just going to do his room upstairs.

He'll feel more in touch with things, Madeleine said: and it'll be easier to move him in and out. If he wants to sit outdoors sometimes or eat with us.

Madeleine's hands seized the pillow and held it to her in a quick embrace. She squeezed it, shook it, plumped it up. Tenderly she laid it on the bed. Her hands went to the sheets again. They stroked, smoothed. The sheets lay back, flat, unresistant.

I was going to do that, Thérèse said: I thought of that.

Madeleine was wearing a dress Thérèse hadn't seen before. Yellow piqué with little cap sleeves. Wedge-heeled white sandals completed her outfit. She'd painted her toenails red.

Nothing more to do in here, Madeleine said: that's it, finished.

She indicated the vase of daisies on the table by the bed, the pile of books, the radio. She put her hands on her jaunty yellow hips, patted the crisp flare of her skirts. She smiled at Thérèse.

If you want to help, perhaps you'd give Victorine a hand with washing up the breakfast things? I want to get on with preparing lunch. I want to have everything ready in good time.

I want to make lunch, Thérèse said: let me do it.

The white bed looked very comfortable and cool. Madeleine gave it one more glance, then shooed Thérèse out in front of her.

Are you sure you'll be able to manage? she asked: I thought you loathed cooking. It's fish. D'you know how to do it?

Of course, Thérèse said.

Well, Madeleine fussed: if you're sure.

Thérèse triumphed. She hustled Victorine and Madeleine from the kitchen, then tied on an apron and set to. For some reason she felt like crying. She held the feeling in tight, she squashed it down under the heavy pasteboard covers of the recipe book. Her tears died like a flattened insect, quick smear on the table-top.

She decided to make a herb sauce to go with the cold poached mackerel, rather than the mayonnaise Madeleine had planned. Tastier, more original. Her father might fancy that. She'd coax him to try a bit. Egg yolks mixed with Dijon mustard, thickened with both melted butter and olive oil, flavoured with tarragon.

She fetched a handful of the aniseed-smelling leaves from the kitchen-garden, stripped them, limp and thin, from their stems. She began to mince them into a fragrant green hill on the board in front of her. She tried to pray for her father at the same time, but Madeleine danced across her invocation, Madeleine provocative in yellow piqué and high-heeled sandals disrupted her holy words.

A correct *liaison* between the egg yolks and the butter is obtained, Madeleine cooed: incorrect. A liaison.

Thérèse shook her head, to clear it. Madeleine vanished. From the curdled phrases sprang a message.

Fetch your mother's letters and read them.

That hoard of words was still in the biscuit tin at the back of the *buffet*. Unless stupid interfering Madeleine had found it and removed it.

Louis was the King, and Thérèse was his little queen. He'd always called her that. Till he got ill, and lost his speech. When he gets well again, Thérèse thought: Madeleine won't let him remember, she doesn't know the right words to say.

Little flower. Little queen. Madeleine picked up the epithets and laughed at them. She dropped them on the chopping-board and crushed them under the blade of her knife. She sniffed them, wrinkled up her nose in disgust. Thérèse shouted out the Holy Name of Jesus and wiped Madeleine from her mind, wiped her hands on her apron. She ran to the dining-room and opened the doors of the *buffet*. She took out the tin box of letters and carried it back with her into the kitchen.

Thérèse knew that she had been sent away from her parents at the age of two months, to be fed by Rose, that she had lived with Rose for sixteen months. It wasn't a secret. Antoinette had once or twice talked of it, and Thérèse herself had one or two dim memories of that time. A shallow stone sink in the corner where Rose unbuttoned the front of her dress to wash herself. The brown of her sunburned arms that ended above her elbows, abruptly as gloves, the startling white of her shoulders and breast.

There was a secret somewhere, though, that Thérèse had to get hold of and understand. Secrets were what lay underneath. Like when a woman slowly unbuttoned her yellow clothes, let them fall down around her waist. While Louis watched. It was disgusting. Antoinette was pure. Surely she would never have behaved like that.

Thérèse was fishing out letters at random, glancing at them while she worked. Antoinette's cool voice sounded faintly in her imagination. As though she were buried under layers of white leaves.

Do you mind that I continue to call you Marie-Jo? You're still my sister, after all! I feel so close to you. But now that *this* has happened I'll never be able to join you in the convent. My dream of the religious life is shattered. I'm so ashamed.

The letters sounded as though they were weeping, Thérèse thought.

Those filthy Germans. Destroying everything. Taking everything they've a mind to. Overfamiliarity. Illbred.

Too much for Thérèse to take in at one go. She dropped the flimsy pages on to the table-top, concentrated on whisking two egg yolks in a china bowl. Her poor father might still like his lunch on time, even though he could no longer hold a fork and had to be helped to eat. She had watched Madeleine feed him in hospital, patiently push soup between his lips. A man turned into a baby, who bobbed his head and wept. But a man still, who could betray one woman with another.

Words from the letters banged about in Thérèse's head, just above her eyebrows she pictured them, as she dripped melted butter from the little saucepan on to the yellow puddle of egg yolks. Cellar. Hiding it. He found me. Dark. Held. Couldn't escape.

She put down the saucepan, prodded the pile of letters, tugged one out from farther down.

Léonie's turned out the difficult one, the neat script ran on: I tell Madeleine she should be stricter with her but of course I mustn't criticize her too much. She's got English ways that's all. Spoils that child. But I'll never forget how good she was to me all through the war, took so much off my hands when I just couldn't cope. I'm worried about Léonie, who's been sleepwalking again. Up and down she goes, talking gibberish. You can imagine what it reminds me of, it's terribly upsetting. But Madeleine won't let me wake her up, she insists on waiting until she goes back to bed of her own accord. I think we should tie her in, but Madeleine won't hear of it. But it solved the problem of Thérèse's tantrums at night, it cured them in no time.

I had a very happy childhood! Thérèse called out to the wooden spoon clotted with Dijon mustard. She banged it on the chopping-board. Mustard splashed about. One big drop hit a letter, sank in, an oily stain on the crinkled paper. She dotted her forefinger into a thick yellow pool on the table-top, licked it, winced at its fiery and concentrated taste. Her mind was as hot as the mustard, words wanting to spill out, dirty the front of a yellow piqué dress.

What did he do is Léonie really my sister what did he do?

The questions swam about the kitchen. Not calm and cool like poached mackerel. This was a school of monster fish, hungrily alive. Baring their white teeth and smiling.

Thérèse mopped up the mustard, swept the chopped tarragon into the mayonnaise, mixed it well together. She could not get the image of a yellow piqué dress crumpled on a white bed out of her mind.

The love of human beings, Thérèse knew from the lives of the saints, was unreliable and let you down. Only God, as she'd found out herself, was an inexhaustible source of love. He never failed you. Even when he hid in the darkness he was just teasing. You could be sure he was there. He never went away. He simply waited for sinners to return to him. And sometimes, as had happened to her last Sunday in church, he came in person and snatched them up in his everlasting arms.

Go to the woods.

Thérèse started. The voice came from inside or outside? She didn't care. What mattered was obeying it. Her conviction that the Virgin was calling her was so strong that she felt able to defy the priest.

She would go back to the shrine. And perhaps the Virgin would be there.

She snatched at the strings of her apron, fingers fretting at the lumpy knot in the small of her back. She hung the apron over the back of a chair, shoved the sauce under a covering plate, turned off the gas under the fish-kettle in which herb-scented water had begun to simmer. I'll only be gone for half an hour or so, she reassured herself: plenty of time to finish it all when I get back. She opened the back door and ran across the yard.

THE DUST

*L*éonie did not want to see the ambulance from the clinic
arrive. She kept clear of everybody in the house in case
they reminded her of the ill person her uncle had become. At first
she hovered in the farmyard, then she wandered over to the stables
and sat on the outside steps up to Louis's workroom. From here she
could see into the fields. Cows grazed with a placid slapping of jaws.
Leaves parted from the beech trees, whirled in eddies of wind. She
was seated in blue sky, the clouds at her back, hearing the church
bells roll out the quarter-hour. Thérèse, rushing across the back yard,
didn't notice her. She vanished at full tilt towards the kitchen-garden
and the orchards. Then Baptiste appeared.

He strolled, hands in pockets, whistling. Was obviously pretending he didn't know she was there. Léonie sat up straight,
tucked her feet to one side, put her hands round her knees. Her
stomach had gone all loose. Baptiste was standing on the bottom
step of the wooden staircase, affecting surprise at the sight of
her.

Oh. Hello. Where's Thérèse?

Léonie managed to reply: hello.

Then she added: I don't know. I haven't seen her.

Both stared at the ground. At least he'd stopped calling her an
English pig. Baptiste coughed and she looked up.

He said: I've got something to show you. Come and see. Then you
can tell Thérèse.

What is it?

I'm not telling you. Come and see.

Léonie stood up. She straightened the skirt that Thérèse had lent
her, dusted it with both hands, then descended the stairs.

It's in your house, Baptiste said: upstairs. My mother told me about it. Let's go and see.

Léonie stood still.

My uncle.

They won't take any notice of us, Baptiste said: the ambulance is round the front, I saw it, and they're carrying him into the downstairs bit. You've got a backstairs haven't you?

She'd done this so often with Thérèse. Slipping in without the grown-ups noticing. Not necessarily *en route* to mischief. Simply the pleasure of not being seen and bothered with. Up the backstairs in bare feet so that no one would hear and interrupt them. Baptiste was trying to take the lead, but that wouldn't do. He didn't know the house, didn't know which doors and floorboards creaked. She motioned him with her head and he swung in behind. This was a betrayal of Thérèse all right. Letting Baptiste in where the two of them had reigned together for so long. She wanted to do it. To hurt Thérèse back for robbing her of the lady in the woods. She would show her. So she beckoned to Baptiste and he crept up the stairs after her, his shoes in his hand.

She paused in the doorway leading to the grey corridor that ran across the back of the house.

Where to now then?

Baptiste looked about. Clearly doing calculations in his head. Screwing up his eyes as he attempted to remember what Rose had said. He pointed.

In there. Maman said it was at the back, the other way from the bathroom end of the corridor.

It can't be, Léonie said: not in there. What is it anyway?

She leaned against the door of her old room. The one she had slept in for years before moving upstairs this summer to share with Thérèse. There was nothing in this room she didn't know. No secrets. It was too bare and plain for that.

It was just around the time you were born, Baptiste said: I don't remember it either. I was too young.

They stood close together on the wooden floor. Carpet and bits of furniture were gone. Sunlight fell across the windowsill, on to their feet. There was a closed smell. Stuffiness and dust.

My parents hid the Jews in their apple loft for two months, Baptiste said: then when the Germans found them they locked them up in here. On the night before they took them out to be shot. They did it on purpose, Maman says. To make people think someone in the Martin family was the informer. They chose this room because it's nearest the backstairs. They weren't going to have Jews using the front ones.

Somewhere a massive pendulum swung to and fro. It counted the minutes before the dawn. There was no escape from it. So heavy it would crush you as it pushed from side to side. It was the blood in Léonie's chest. Her heart pumped so strongly she felt she'd burst. There was a heartbeat in her neck, in her head, on her tongue.

The Jews, the Jews, she said: didn't they have names then?

Some foreign name, Baptiste said: Maman told it me but I can't remember. She said she always used their false name anyway, never their real one. They weren't from round here. They were refugees from Rouen.

He struck a heroic attitude. Like one of the soldiers on the war memorial rallying *La République* with fixed bayonets.

Those pigs of Germans shot my father. *Vive la France!*

Léonie pointed her toe and wrote an imaginary signature in the dust. Then she looked at Baptiste. Her blood was slowing down, but her head still felt strange. Full of something thick. Dizzy with the memory of bad dreams.

Did they keep your father in here too? she asked: before he was shot?

Baptiste nodded.

You know what, he said in a rush: at the funeral the Monday before last, they buried my father and the Jews all together in the same grave in the cemetery, they couldn't tell whose bones were whose.

He sounded ashamed.

Monsieur le Curé said the sooner we buried them properly the better, he's not going to tell anyone. So no one can make a fuss. Jews might if they found out. So we're just going to have a plain headstone, with my father's names and dates. *Monsieur le Curé* said he'd pay for it.

Léonie frowned. Something was wrong with this rattled-off speech. Too much of it, perhaps. A pile of leftover words. Scraps of words, old bones of words. Like the sawed bloodied pieces of shin and gristle in the butcher's, shoved into a sacking bag and taken home to feed the dogs. That's what a grave was: a dump for torn flesh, broken bones. The Jews were back in the ground again. Mixed up more than ever before. She wanted to laugh. She felt sick. She leaned on the handle of the door. Coldness of brass, that was solid, refreshing. Grown-ups' secrets. She was sick of them.

She shouldn't have to be bothered. She was only a girl, she was too young.

I'll show you how to juggle if you like, she told Baptiste: come downstairs and we'll get some potatoes off Victorine and I'll show you how to juggle.

Magic tricks. To make things vanish you threw them in the air then cooked and ate them. You could do it with bones too. Léonie left the Jews behind her in the room. She closed the door on them. They could not escape, but she could. She was a mongrel, only half-French, but she wasn't Jewish. She had a larder with baskets of potatoes, she would not starve, she would not burn.

Victorine was in the kitchen, ripping the silvery-blue skin off mackerel. The air was warm with the scent of hot fish stock, *bouquet garni*. The biscuit tin supported the open recipe book.

Where's Thérèse? Victorine cried out as soon as she saw them: that wretched child, I knew it would be hopeless letting her help, it's too much, I'll never be done in time.

She swivelled her eyes to the potatoes Léonie was fetching from their earthy resting-place on the larder floor.

Good idea. You get on with them. Baptiste, run and ask your mother to come and give me a hand, would you?

Léonie felt comfortable again. Back with what she knew. She watched Victorine lay the cooling fillets one by one on a flat dish. The bones lifted off easily, a spiky white all-in-one. Victorine tossed them into the plastic waste bowl that stood by the side of the sink. She ladled a little of the *court bouillon* over the fat bits of mackerel. Peppercorns and parsley, a good fish and white wine stink. She threw her ladle down. It clanged against the biscuit tin.

What on earth is that box of biscuits doing out at this time of day? Victorine shouted: go on, put it away will you? Hurry up. Then come back and we'll make a start on the potatoes.

It isn't biscuits, Léonie said: it's letters. Thérèse's. I'd better not move it or she'll think it's lost.

Victorine's voice softened.

She's probably crept in to be with her father. His first day back after all. It's what you'd expect.

THE BLUE SKIRT

*T*hérèse came to slowly. Sunlight dazzling through the trees forced her eyelids open. She brought her outstretched arms down, clasped her hands together. The light rested on her cheeks as heavily as tears. The people kneeling around her sighed all together, a breath of wonder that rippled through them. Wind over the wheat, she thought: over the leaves on the vine. The bread and the wine. The harvest's gifts. Those were the words she had to remember. The bread and the wine.

Behind her she heard the Bishop's voice.

That little girl's no fake. I don't know when I've seen anything so heavenly as that gesture of welcome she made, that smile that she mirrored.

Thérèse came to kneel at his feet. She hitched up her new blue skirt to avoid dirtying it. Her bare knees met muddy grass, stones. The Bishop's shoes were black and shiny as hearses. The Bishop's hand, with its jewelled gold ring, was extended for her to kiss. Beside him stood the village priest, his face carefully bland.

What an exquisite honour, remarked the priest: that our little ceremony of blessing should be graced with the presence of Our Lady. Really so completely unexpected!

He glared at Thérèse. She bowed her head to the Bishop's purple and gold. The blue and silver glow of the vision had pushed him out of her consciousness, but now she saw him she had to admit how very handsome and grand he was in his mitre and robes.

He said: well child, what has Our Lady got to say to me?

His eyes were wrinkled up. Perhaps against the sun. But they looked wet. He wanted something, a share in what she'd seen. Everyone did. That was why the small crowd of villagers stood near, to catch a word, an expression on her face, to touch her hand or sleeve. Not as many as had first come, of course. These country people did not love bishops, the paraphernalia of church hierarchy. Still, enough of them were present to make sure the Virgin's message would be spread all round the village by supper-time.

The Bishop was taller than Thérèse, yet, even kneeling, she had the sensation of looking down on him. With tenderness. Poor man, shut out, as they all were except her, from that glimpse of heaven's dazzling sweetness. At the same time he was a great lord. With real power in the world. If he commanded then people jumped to do his bidding.

She raised her eyes shyly. She clasped her hands.

She said: Our Blessed Lady asked me to ask you to have a small chapel built here in her honour. On this spot where the shrine was before. She wants a statue set up inside the chapel. She wants to be known as Our Lady of Blémont-la-Fontaine, and her feast-day is to be in early September on the day we have the harvest festival.

A demanding lot, these women, murmured the *curé*: they don't ask much!

The Bishop smiled.

After all, it may be for the best. In all ways. A sign of the renewal of faith in these dark materialistic times.

He put his hand under Thérèse's chin and made her rise. He stared into her face. She blushed faintly and gazed back. He patted her cheek. Raised his hand to bless her. As she made the sign of the cross he spoke in loud and solemn tones.

Tell the lady next time you see her that she can have her chapel. I am convinced it will do nothing but good.

He turned to the *curé*.

My dear Father, you were mentioning lunch?

Thérèse clapped her hand to her mouth.

I must go. I'm cooking fish for lunch for my father. He's come home today from hospital.

The Bishop took off his mitre and handed it to an adjacent altar-boy. He ran his hand through his flattened hair.

Fish? What kind of fish?

Fish soup with *rouille*, Thérèse said: followed by poached mackerel with *sauce à l'estragon*.

I shall come and lunch with your family, the Bishop declared: nothing formal, eh? A simple meal *en famille*. I feel I must meet, as part of my pastoral duties, the noble father of such a modest little visionary.

He turned to the priest at his side.

My dear Father. You will accompany me of course. Your faithful housekeeper can have the day off. I shall enjoy her admirable turnip stew another time.

He waved his beringed hand at Thérèse.

Run along child. We'll be with you at one o'clock sharp.

She ran.

THE SLOTTED SPOON

Rose and Victorine reacted to the word *Bishop* in a practical way. They sped off to the dining-room to organize putting an extra leaf in the table. Thérèse strolled from the back door over to the stove where the fish-kettle still stood, awash with cooking juice. She dipped a finger in, licked it.

Isn't lunch ready yet? she enquired.

Léonie peered at her. She was pink-cheeked, smiling. But she wouldn't catch Léonie's eye. She hummed a tune and pretended to care about tasting a fragment of fish she'd pinched up out of the herby broth. Léonie waited a second. Then she pulled the biscuit tin towards her across the table, yanked off the lid. She lifted a sheet of writing and studied it. Thérèse hurriedly wiped her hand against her mouth, lunged for the letter.

Leave it alone! They're mine!

She scrambled the piece of paper back into its sugar-and-vanilla-scented tin box. She held the lid as though it were a tambourine.

I don't think you should read them. You haven't, have you? You'd be upset.

Léonie was alert. She reflected. She blurted out her offer.

I'll tell you my secret if you'll tell me yours.

Thérèse asked: what secret? I'm not interested in Baptiste if that's what you mean.

She jerked her chin at the box of letters.

Go on then. Read them if you want to. Read the ones on top first. Only don't say I didn't warn you.

When shall I tell you my secret then? Léonie asked.

Thérèse shrugged.

Oh. I don't care. It'll keep I expect.

She picked up a slotted spoon from the table and beat gently on the tin lid.

What have you done with the sauce I made? It was here when I went out, I left it here. In a bowl. Under a plate.

In the fridge of course, Léonie said: if you mean that tarragon stuff.

She was exasperated. But she felt she had to obey Thérèse. Choosing a letter would have to be done on the same principle as choosing a biscuit. Good manners forbade you to riffle through the pile, lift the layers until you found one you liked the look of. You took what your hostess offered. So Léonie plucked out the letter Thérèse indicated, the one that she had replaced on top. December 1941. Antoinette to Sœur Dosithée. Her eyes wandered around the loops and curlicues of the writing. She began to read.

Thérèse laughed. She was dancing the slotted spoon in and out of the fish-kettle, a clatter of aluminium.

You call this stuff fish soup? I'd better do something about improving it. Can't give this to the Bishop. What can Madeleine be thinking of?

Léonie lifted her head.

We made the soup while you were out. It's in the larder, so the cats don't get at it. I was just going to wash up the kettle when you came in.

Too good to waste, Thérèse said.

She poured the leftover liquid into a small bowl. She drank it thirstily, holding back the bits of herb and onion with a teaspoon. She watched Léonie finish reading the letter.

THE WASHING-UP BOWL

M adeleine and Victorine had dressed Louis in his best blue jersey for lunch. The stroke had flattened and aged him. His body had become plump and loose. His hands dangled over the sides of the wheelchair as they took him to the *salon* to meet the Bishop. He was like a middle-aged child, puzzled and sweet, his blue eyes full of tears. His hair, which had not been cut for weeks, fell in silky waves around his face.

The priest and the Bishop stood in front of the fireplace, looking down at him. Madeleine and Victorine stood behind his wheelchair, like nurses, while the two girls huddled on the windowseat. Rose came in with a tray of glasses and bottles. The two clerics brightened up, and accepted a whisky each.

At lunch Louis was wedged, lolling, into his chair. He peered over a rampart of cushions. Madeleine fastened his napkin around his neck. She pegged it on to his blue jersey with the tiny plastic clothes-pins she used for hanging up her dripping stockings in the bathroom to dry overnight. She sat next to him so that she could cut up his food and discreetly help his wavering hand shove it into his mouth. From time to time he dribbled and then wept tears of rage and humiliation. The guests looked the other way and talked more loudly.

Thérèse sat with lowered eyes. Looking like a sort of holy pig, Léonie thought. Too rapt in awe of the Bishop to bother with her food. She dipped her spoon into her plate of fish soup as though it were gutter water she was forcing herself to swallow, and she wouldn't take any of the little circles of toast spread with delicious fiery *rouille*. The Bishop nodded his approval of this asceticism before accepting the offer of a second helping from Madeleine. The lid lifted off the tureen. The fragrance of fish, tomato and garlic gushed out.

Léonie followed his example and had some more too. She eyed the last piece of toast and *rouille*, decided she didn't dare look as though she wanted it. Today she was on best behaviour. She'd put on a dress for lunch. The Bishop reached out a casual hand and took it. Madeleine smiled her satisfaction.

The two girls' job was to clear the table between courses, fetch and carry dishes. They ferried plates to and fro from the kitchen, where Rose and Victorine supervised what was to come next. They'd taken no notice of Thérèse reporting that the Bishop expected only a simple meal. They'd got out the best china and crystal glasses, the damask napkins, the ebony-handled knives. The best cider for the Bishop, and the best wine. Certainly the Bishop did not seem impatient of the efforts expended on his behalf. He praised the poached mackerel and its delicate herb-scented sauce. He accepted a third glass of Muscadet. He raised it to the blushing Thérèse.

My compliments, child, on your cooking.

She looked at him imploringly.

God isn't calling me to be a cook, Your Excellency, he's calling me to be a contemplative. Please, Your Excellency, I beg of you, give me your permission to enter the convent as soon as I'm sixteen.

The Bishop roared with laughter.

Absurd child. That's far too young. Wait until you're eighteen and then we'll see.

Louis turned his head towards his daughter, his tongue protruding as he tried to speak, failed, wept. She swivelled her face from his. She smiled at the Bishop.

Really Thérèse, Madeleine scolded her: to upset him like that on his first day at home! How dare you talk such nonsense!

The Bishop wiped a speck of sauce from his chin.

Not nonsense, my dear *Madame*. A religious vocation is the highest call anyone may receive. And for a young girl who has been privileged to see, with the eyes of her soul, the Mother of Our Lord, it is perhaps the only vocation that she should contemplate. That those eyes which have witnessed the Divine Motherhood should henceforward be for ever lowered in contemplation in an enclosed cloister seems to me entirely fitting. Heaven forbid that this child should ever be tainted by the grossness of the world!

Madeleine mopped Louis's eyes with the corner of his napkin. She murmured to him and put her hand over his.

A good religious boarding-school, the *curé* announced: that might be the answer for now. For certainly, once the chapel is built and consecrated, there will be pilgrims coming from all over Normandy. The shrine may become famous throughout France. Who knows, perhaps we'll even see a miracle or two.

He beamed at Thérèse.

To me, dear child, you confided your secret. To me you told the story of the apparitions. As your parish priest, it is my duty to shield you from any overenthusiasm on the part of visitors hoping to catch a glimpse of a visionary. We must remember how much poor Saint Bernadette suffered. A boarding-school, that is undoubtedly the best course for now.

Léonie, Madeleine said: go and fetch the salad will you?

The Bishop peered at her.

Léonie. Yes. I heard tales, let me see, about a second child having visions, of a somewhat different sort?

Completely discredited, the *curé* said: a most unfortunate mistake. She's half-English I'm afraid. There was a mix-up of languages. A problem of translation. She was trying to report what Thérèse told her and she got it wrong.

Léonie waited for her mother to laugh and assert that her daughter spoke perfect French. But Madeleine didn't seem to have heard. She was stroking Louis's cheek and whispering to him reassuringly. Her pet, to be slipped titbits and fondled when no one was looking. What kind of pet? Léonie got up after a moment and went out to get the salad.

After the *dessert* and the fruit came the coffee. Leaving the men and Madeleine sipping Calvados and smoking, the two girls brushed the crumbs off the glossy white cloth and took themselves to the kitchen. Victorine and Rose had gone, leaving tottering piles of dirty plates, cutlery soaking in jugs, saucepans and pots lined up at the side of the sink.

Léonie and Thérèse did the washing-up together. Léonie, with her sleeves rolled up and Victorine's big blue overall wrapped round her, held the smeared plates under the hot tap, dunked them into the soapy water in the yellowing plastic bowl in the enamel sink, stacked them in the wooden rack on the tin draining-board. Thérèse, armed with a thin red and white linen cloth, dried, polished, sorted.

At first they did not speak to each other. Léonie tried, but each time she opened her mouth an invisible hand blocked it and shut her up. What it was that wanted to come out she did not know. An animal's yelp of pain or a shriek of amusement. She clutched the soft sponge in her palm, feathery with water and soap. She let the cooling suds tickle her wrists, worked her white-locked mop in and out of glasses.

Thérèse picked with her fingernail at a crust of grease in the bottom of a saucepan. Still she kept silence. Then she could not restrain herself, pounced with a sharp cry on a smear under the handle of the colander. Léonie grabbed both pots back, rebaptized them in a squirt of lemony green goo, hot water.

Holy holy holy, she sang: Lord God of Bishops. Thérèse you can't mean it, you're not really going to go and be a nun?

Thérèse swabbed the lid of the saucepan. Thin and battered, made of tin, with a wooden button to lift it by.

I am. You and Madeleine will go on living here. You can look after Papa. You don't need me.

Léonie upended her bowl and let the water swish round the sink. It left a tidemark of greasy bits as it sank away down the plughole.

We're never going back to England? How d'you know?

Thérèse folded her tea-towel and hung it on the silver bar in front of the range.

Madeleine's going to marry Papa, isn't she? It's obvious. It's far too soon but still. Don't be stupid. Use your eyes. It's really sick and disgusting I think, she should be ashamed of herself.

Thérèse's eyes glittered. They said: grow up. Don't make one single sound of grief. Pain squatted Thérèse, Léonie could see. A stretch, an ache. But her voice was cool and light.

I'd like to go to the missions abroad, Thérèse mused: that would be the most exciting. Real adventures. The African bush. Danger. But my vocation might be to enter the convent here in Normandy. It's hard to tell. I'll have to pray for guidance.

Did saints ever bat their eyelids and look sleepily self-satisfied as cats? Thérèse, lowering her lashes like a lacy brown veil and trying not to smile too obviously, did not look modest. It was the same look she'd directed at the men all through lunch and they'd loved it. Léonie thought men were stupid to be so easily taken in. Look flutteringly at them, pout with all your maidenly charm, above all don't say a word, and they were yours. She vowed that never would she resort to such cheap tricks. She would die rather than roll her eyes and wriggle and blush.

God speaks to me, Thérèse said: I can't explain it, you wouldn't understand.

Why not, Léonie cried out: why wouldn't I?

You're the sort of girl, Thérèse pronounced: who'll probably not have much of a career. You'll get married very young I expect. You're a bit of a tart really aren't you. Like Madeleine.

And you're not I suppose, Léonie shouted: just a holy tart, making eyes at the Bishop to feel important. God I hate you Thérèse Martin.

Thérèse picked up the biscuit box from the table. Her voice was calm but her hand shook.

Unchastity is a mortal sin. It means you go to hell. My poor mother. It's even worse than what happened to Saint Maria Goretti. At least *she* died defending her honour. It was the only thing she could do. It's worse when you don't die. Everybody whispers about you. It's disgusting.

Thérèse's eyes glared in her pale face. Sweat from the washing-up misted her forehead and nose.

I don't know what you're talking about, Léonie lied: I don't know what's the matter with you.

Thérèse clasped the biscuit tin in the crook of her arm.

It was a terrible sin, she said: which means we've got to pray for forgiveness. To make reparation. You ask Madeleine. She'll have to admit it, it's all true.

She won't tell me anything, Léonie said: she never does. Did she tell you?

She didn't need to, Thérèse said: it's all there, in the letters. Of course we were never meant to find out.

She was trying not to cry.

They've betrayed me. I don't want you as my sister. I want Papa.

She didn't care what Léonie felt. She didn't care who was watching. She wrenched the lid off the biscuit tin and tipped her mother's letters into the range, stuffing them well down with the poker until there was nothing left of them but black ash.

Explain to me, Léonie cried: tell me what you mean.

THE VASE

*A*fter the lunch guests had gone the house settled down into quiet. Louis slept in his bed in the little white *salon*. Madeleine sat and sewed next door. Within earshot in case he woke and needed her. Thérèse had stormed off towards the village.

Léonie didn't know where to put herself and the knowledge dumped on her by Thérèse. This secret could not be shared with the grown-ups. They had kept it all these years. They would be distraught if they discovered that now she and Thérèse *knew*. Better to keep quiet, protect them. The words stuck in her throat, like a large crumb, or a grape-pip she wanted to spit out and couldn't.

She wandered into the dining-room. So empty and undisturbed you couldn't imagine the bustle of the lunch party only an hour before. Chairs decorously ranged in their places, the white cloth gone. A faint scent of tobacco and fish lingered, even though one of the windows had been opened. The thin white curtain, pulled back, fluttered in the cool air. The only sound was the soft tick of the tall clock in the corner, the cooing of pigeons and doves outside.

Mother. Father. All you had to go on was what they told you. You had to believe that Madeleine told the truth. Now you suspected she'd been lying to you for thirteen years.

She felt clumsy, too big. She put out a hand to touch one of the ribbed blue and yellow vases on the marble mantelpiece. Easy to break it. Thin, hollow porcelain. Fragile. She wanted the vase to lift up and off, potter through the air in a slow-motion arc, sprinkle itself in tinkling bits on the glazed tiles surrounding the empty fireplace.

She shouted inside herself to Thérèse: I don't want you to be my sister either so there, see if *I* care.

She jammed her fists into her pockets. Her surprised fingers encountered something hard. A sharp earthenware edge. She brought it out to look at it. The fragment of the Quimper dish she had picked up from the dustpan on the kitchen floor that day when she and Thérèse had seen, when she saw, when the lady had shown herself for the second time. She'd hidden her stolen relic at the back of the bedroom cupboard in the pocket of this dress that she hardly ever wore. Then she'd forgotten all about it.

The painted hands of the Quimper lady, joined about her tiny posy of flowers, were severed at the wrist. What had her face looked like? Léonie could not remember. She curled her fingers around the shard in her palm, slipped it back into the thin pouch of cotton hidden inside the skirts of her dress. Then she went over to the *buffet* and stood in front of it. She traced with her forefinger the silky whorls of the carved garland of oak leaves that swung across both doors.

The only thing to do was to go for a walk. She ambled towards the orchards, the boundary wall.

The small green space in the centre of the woods looked like a chapel already. People had piled the fallen stones into the shape of an altar, and had put a white lace-edged cloth on top. On this were arranged thick candles in red glass jars, two vases of dahlias, a small plaster statue of Our Lady. Strips of old carpet had been laid down in rows, like pews. Scattered about was exactly the sort of clutter you found in the parish church: holy pictures of saints, missals, rosaries, little bottles of holy water.

Léonie curled up on one of the bits of carpet. She laid her head on her arm. She squinted. Yes. It was Baptiste, walking across the clearing and lowering himself to sit next to her. Everybody else in the village was presumably either still eating lunch or else dozing. There were just the two of them. The hairs on his forearm brushed hers, he sat so close.

He said: I thought you were asleep.

Léonie shook her head. Doing this dislodged the words stuck in her throat. They flew about inside her like magpies in an orchard, then settled in a new pattern. When she opened her mouth they darted out, glossy and black and white.

She said: Thérèse has found out that she and I are really sisters, not cousins. Twins. My mother's really my aunt. She adopted me. She's not my mother at all.

Baptiste looked stupefied. He was lipreading as well as listening. Needing all his wits to follow her. Failing.

What? What did you say?

I'm not half-English at all, Léonie said: Maurice wasn't my father. They just told me he was. They lied to me.

Baptiste tugged out a thread from the edge of the carpet. He rolled it into a ball, put it into his mouth, chewed.

Thérèse is crazy. She's made it up. It's just one of her mad stories. Like seeing the Virgin Mary.

Léonie frowned. Baptiste spat out his bit of thread and laughed.

So you're not *half*-French. You're *French*. Now that suits you much better. Little French girl.

He rolled his rrrs to make her laugh too. Léonie sprawled lower on the muddy carpet and looked up at the beech trees spread against the sky.

She said: Thérèse says it was in the war. After people hid their cider and wine from the Germans in our cellar. They covered the bottles with a great heap of sand.

I know that, Baptiste protested: everyone knows that. Try telling me a story I don't know!

The sky and the trees pressed down on to Léonie's face. She recited. Words that were not hers. They tripped out neat and pat. Arranged in rows like magpies on a fence.

Thérèse says it was all there in the letters she got back from the convent. One of the Germans stationed in the house got suspicious of Antoinette hanging about near the cellar door and made her give him the key and go down there with him so he could see what she was hiding. Then later on she found she was going to have a baby.

It's a story, Baptiste declared: she got from some stupid women's magazine or other. You're telling me she gave herself to the German to stop him finding the wine? She seduced him?

Léonie's arms and legs dissolved with relief now the words were out, had flown off squawking.

Thérèse says the letters didn't put it very clearly. You could hardly say that to a nun could you? But that's what they *meant*.

Half-French and half-*German*? Baptiste enquired.

He examined her, as though her skin, her eyelashes, her hair, could tell the whole truth and nothing but the truth. He wouldn't like her so much now. It was all Thérèse's fault.

Antoinette married Louis, Léonie explained: so that everyone would think the baby was his. She'd been thinking about becoming a nun but she couldn't be with a baby. Then when she had twins she gave one to her married sister. That was me.

It didn't matter. Nothing mattered. She kept her head down, let her mouth brush the fibres of the carpet, caked with mud and dust. When Baptiste's hand touched her arm she jumped.

You're not half-German, he said: I don't believe it. It's a pack of lies.

Baptiste lay down beside her. His mouth brushed her ear.

What do *you* think happened?

The end of Thérèse's story was that Antoinette had been found out. Proof: her stomach had swelled. Shame brought upon her family. Outrage. Disgrace.

Léonie turned her head so that she could look at Baptiste. She was pleased at how low her voice was, how steady.

Oh, I think I'm wholly French, she said: I've been working it out. I don't think it was a German soldier at all. I'm sure Thérèse made that up. I think it was Louis all along.

For Louis, Antoinette had kicked off her buttoned high-heeled shoes by the wine racks and lain down on gritty sand. Was it better to be raped by a Nazi than seduced by a Frenchman? Would you be forgiven quicker? The priest would say neither. But anyway Antoinette had had to get married. She'd been found out.

The pain burrowed through Léonie, tore at her with sharp claws. She'd been cast out, first by one woman and then by another. Tossed between them like a broken toy fit only for the dustbin. Really it was all Thérèse's fault. She'd insisted on telling Léonie. She'd taken everything from her. Then she'd said they were sisters. Like a slap. Léonie would scratch back. Rescue herself. She wouldn't be caught, trapped in the darkness. She wasn't a Jew. It wasn't her fault. She was French.

Ripping off her Englishness and casting it aside was as easy as unfastening the collar of her dress. Her fingers glided over the frilled edges of daisy-shaped buttons. Shaking off the very idea of a German father was a wriggle of the shoulders, the thin cotton sleeves pushed down. Becoming French was taking Thérèse as her twin sister and then taking the boy she wanted. Baptiste, baptism, his tongue sliding into her mouth and blessing her, she wanted to laugh, she kissed him back. Thérèse could share in this, they were sisters weren't they, in the past they'd shared everything, food games beds a sack of skin.

Léonie wanted to be found out. She wanted to find out what it was like, Antoinette in the cellar, Madeleine in the big marital bed, their mysterious life in the arms of men, the embrace which the daughter was banned from and which they told endless lies about. Poor stupid ignorant lying Thérèse. Let her find out too. What it felt like to be left out.

Léonie opened one eye and cocked it ready. She opened her knees, drew Baptiste to her, held him firmly with both hands. She saw colours stir, a flash of black amongst the greenery. She waited for the shouts from beyond the trees, for the priest and the Bishop and Thérèse to come running, to come upon this sinful worship on the ground.

THE CIGARETTE

More than twenty years later Thérèse had returned home to lie in the bed in which she'd been born and to quarrel with Léonie. She longed for sleep, to muffle her ears against Léonie's shrill voice, implacable words that spattered her skin like pellets of ice. She crossed her arms and shivered. She cowered under the gaze of the woman opposite her, who threatened the air with a cigarette. As though the air had sinned, becoming too stale and smoke-filled. In this hectic mood Léonie was exactly like Antoinette. Did she berate her daughters in these accusing tones? No wonder, Thérèse thought: none of them is at home.

She said: you don't really mean that. You haven't really spent all this time pretending I didn't exist. You're exaggerating because you're upset.

Dead, I said, Léonie corrected her: I said that for twenty years I pretended you were *dead*.

In the convent Thérèse had died to the world. A white death. It had snowed on the day of her clothing. White fringes decorated the windowsills. The sky was a canopy of white held over a bride. When she walked along the cloister on her way to the chapel, the cloister garth spun with whiteness fine as the veil covering her hair. She wished now she could hold the white sheets of her bed in front of her face, to blot out Léonie's furious eyes. Cover her up. Bury her in snow.

You didn't come to my clothing did you, she remarked: you wrote saying you couldn't afford the fare.

Over by the door Léonie rubbed her nose between finger and thumb, then sighed explosively.

I suppose you offered it up for the holy souls, she said: that was what you always used to do.

Madeleine and Louis came, Thérèse said: so why not you?

Léonie paced to and fro in the shadowy space between the bed and the door. She clasped the ashtray in one hand and made half-stifled gestures with the other.

You weren't able to attend their funerals, of course, she said: the convent rules forbade it. I'm sure you offered *that* up as a sacrifice too didn't you? You didn't think about me having to cope completely on my own.

You had Baptiste, Thérèse reminded her: and you also had the house, and the farm.

Inside herself she was held together by knotted strings. One by one Léonie was slicing through them. Soon her arms and legs would fall off, plop, then her head. Léonie's precise strokes with the knife dismembered her. Like a chicken carcase on the kitchen table, joints and sinews severed, skin ripped off then bundled away. Hunched in her bed, Thérèse held on to a pillow and squinted at the other woman. Clearly Léonie found pleasure in this, letting out stored words in a rush, found a warmth and energy. Keen focus. Slapping cut after cut into the flesh of her target, then drawing breath to let fly again. Thérèse never got angry. She'd rooted it out of herself in the early days in the convent, along with all the other feelings that got in God's way. She'd made herself empty as the square plot encircled by the cloisters, open to the silence, the falling snow.

Léonie said: all those lies you tried to make me swallow about Madeleine not being my real mother. About being adopted. About Antoinette being raped by a German. Your big hysterical drama. Just because you were jealous. Your nose put out of joint.

Thérèse flinched. She wanted to protest. She ducked. Her hand flew to her mouth then down again.

Léonie hissed like a cross goose barring the path to the pond with flapping wings. She looked like one, too, plump in shining grey silk, her neck darting forward, all her hair rumpled and on end.

You haven't come back because you care about those dead Jews being dug up out of their burial place, Léonie accused her: you just want to put yourself in the limelight again with some new story. Saint Thérèse the little flower. Our Lady's pet.

I've come back to put the record straight about the past, Thérèse said: I want to admit I made a mistake when I described those visions. I want to tell everyone how sorry I am, for misleading them.

Not a mistake, Léonie said: a lie. You told a lie.

Thérèse glanced up.

You don't care about the dead Jews either, she said: in fact the opposite. All you care about is your position in the village, your nice quiet life. That's all that matters to you. You're a real *bourgeoise* aren't you.

You'll only cause fresh trouble, Léonie cried: nobody'll thank you, you wait and see. We can't live in the past. We've got to get on with our lives.

Hypocrite.

They said the word together. Léonie turned and went out.

THE STATUE

*T*hérèse pushed the window open to get rid of the cigarette smoke, then fell asleep. For the first time since Antoinette's death she dreamed of her.

She and her sisters from the convent, clad in their brown habits, their white coifs and black veils, stood about the table on which Antoinette's body had been put. They were preparing her for burial. They stitched up the torn skin, moulded the features of the face back into position, set the broken bones, then coaxed the limbs to lie straight. The body having been made whole again, they washed and dried it, then wrapped it in a linen sheet. Léonie had been a shadowy figure in the corner, watching in silence. Now she came forward. She made a fist, let sand trickle from it on to the white shroud. She made a pattern. She wrote something, a line of sand. Thérèse craned forward to read it.

She awoke. It was still dark. Her sisters in the convent would be singing the Office at this hour, some of them rubbing the green sleep crusts from the corners of their eyes and stifling yawns, just as she used to, in the choir lit by candles. Far from perfect she'd been, and she'd ended up saying to God: take me as I am, over to you now, I can't do it all by myself.

The practice of twenty years could not easily be abandoned. She sat up, leapt out of bed, fell to her knees. No prayer rose from her heart to her lips. In her mind's eye she saw the edge of a photograph, Léonie smiling behind the lens of a camera. She got up from the floor and dressed, then went quietly downstairs. In her pocket her fingers touched the cigarette lighter that Léonie had left behind on the bedside table.

She went via the main *salon*, so that she could glance at the new photographs tucked into the framed collection hanging above the bureau, the photographs she'd never seen. Léonie and Baptiste on their wedding-day, Léonie in layers of net frills, her hair backcombed into a beehive stuck with orchids, feet encased in shiny white stilettos. Baptiste grinned in a tight dark suit, his bristly hair slicked down and his ears sticking out. Thérèse shook her head over the pair of them. Léonie's teenage rebellion hadn't amounted to much: just a few years of black pullovers and pretending to be a beatnik. She hadn't bothered with higher education. All she cared about, obviously, was her family and her house. The photo of her three daughters was gold-rimmed. A bland portrait of three well-fed *jeunes filles* with ribboned plaits and polite smiles, neatly lined up like some of Léonie's well-dusted china ornaments.

There was no photograph displayed of Thérèse in her habit, on the day of her clothing. Though Madeleine had taken several with Louis's old camera while he looked on, calling out jokes to make Thérèse smile. He'd cried at one point and Thérèse had turned away. Léonie had wiped those memories from the house, like a smudge on a windowpane.

Thérèse found that her knees were shaking.

Get out of here, she thought: but where can I go?

She looked at the photograph of her mother and let the dream sweep back. The mending. The limbs stitched together, the torn pieces reassembled. She looked at Antoinette's calm pale face, at her buttoned high-heeled shoes. She remembered the dark red shoe she'd found in the cellar, behind the barrel, that day with Léonie.

Go back down to the cellar, of course. Antoinette had tried to tell her, as she lay dying, what was down there. But Thérèse had not been able to understand.

The cellar door was unlocked. Thérèse switched on the light and started down the wooden stairs.

The heap of sand, she discovered, was indeed still there. Right at the back, under a low vault, where the light hardly reached and the air was dank. Thérèse knelt down on the earthen floor, pushed her fingers in and moved them about. She made her hands into spades, shovelling the damp grit to one side, digging as deep as she could go.

Her fingernail scratched it. She forced herself to burrow around it, slowly, carefully. She brought it out piece by piece, she brushed the sand from it as best she could, she explored it with her fingertips, she caressed it. A stone leg, stone foot, the pleated dress falling down, exposing the long slender toes. A stone hand clasping a broken sheaf of corn. Half a stone head, one eye slanted, half a curled mouth, tender, amused.

Louis must have helped Antoinette gather up the broken statue and bring it here, Thérèse thought: after the priest smashed it, he must already have been in love with her, else why should he have bothered? He must have helped her to bury it next to the cider and the wine hidden under the sand. Antoinette had been a very pious woman. Just once in her life she'd defied the priest, the Church, acted in a way that allied her to the villagers not just to the big house. No wonder afterwards she'd tried to forget it ever happened. Just one more odd little episode in the war. But Rose and Victorine must also have known, Madeleine too. Perhaps at first they'd simply waited, biding their time until the Germans were gone, then realizing how long they'd have to wait until the hostile young priest retired or moved to another parish. Perhaps, as time went on, it all became less important. Hiding the broken statue had been some sort of daring and romantic game, part of cocking a snook, like cutting off bits of German soldiers' uniforms on trains without being seen, coming home to display scraps of epaulettes, braid. Probably the stone girl's significance had lessened. Local folklore, very nice, but they didn't want any more trouble.

So they'd waited, and they'd forgotten. And the trampled statue had remained in the airless dark, her mouth and nostrils and ears and eyes clogged with dirt and sand. Shut up like a cry in a box, the weight of the house pressing on her.

Yellow stars. A young woman with a dark gold face.

The communal grave. The boulders from the old shrine piled on top of it.

Thérèse thought: Léonie knows all about this, she must do, she'll have had it from Baptiste, who'll have had it from Rose. She's been deliberately not telling me. Her way of punishing me for stealing the lady she saw. But now I've found out.

She dusted off the palms of her hands against her dress and stood up. She left the bits of stone behind her, carefully arranged on the floor, and went back up the stairs into the kitchen. She lifted the latch of the outer door and left the house.

THE
CIGARETTE LIGHTER

Somewhere a dog was asleep, must not be disturbed. Thérèse trod cautiously across the gravel and out of the gate. The light was a milky blue, a heel of white moon showing. The air was fresh and cold, dampening towards rain.

She met no one on the road. Too early, on a Sunday, for people to be about. The village slept behind closed shutters wet with dew. Shops too had their eyelids pulled down. The streets were empty and clean. As though everyone had been evacuated in the night and sent to live somewhere else.

Thérèse shivered in the light wind. While she was on the road night had changed imperceptibly into morning, a grey shift, the sky smudged pink. In this pearly light the façade of the church looked newly washed, yellow as a biscuit.

The door of the church was not locked. Its handle swung forwards, into her hand. She pulled the little door open, and went in.

She remembered the church as a vast, dark place. Edges lost in shadows. Gloomy side-aisles down which you crept on your way back to your pew after receiving communion. Now it seemed small and light, and she could see round it in one glance. Airy, cream-coloured. Stripped. Gone were all the old banners and draperies, the priestly thrones, the tiers of misericords, the carved screens. Gone was the old smell of damp stone and incense and decay. The church smelled of beeswax and grass and flowers.

Thérèse walked slowly up the centre aisle. The pews on either side had been left intact. Worn pine, dark and polished like the *buffet* at home. At the near end of each one, two wooden straw-seated chairs and prie-dieux. Beyond them, in the side aisles, the old statues still occupied their brackets on the wall in between the stained-glass windows. The high altar had been taken away. In its place was a simple stone slab half-covered by a strip of white linen and flanked by pots of yellow dahlias.

The church was all ready for the harvest festival Mass. Decked out as though for a party. The vaulted roof of the nave was crisscrossed by lines of string fringed with sprigs of barley and oats, feathery, fragile. Baskets of wheat and dried blue cornflowers were tied to the columns, to the ends of the pews. Wreaths of wheat were looped over the volutes of the capitals. Larger bouquets, pale gold sprouts, decorated the altar-rails. Bunches of grapes, black and green, dangled from the lectern. Near this stood a three-tiered bier, like a cake-stand, seemingly made entirely of twisted corn. On its lower shelves reposed loaves of bread, bundles of leeks and tomatoes and apples, a basket of corn sprigs tied up with multicoloured ribbons, a straw tray of *brioches*.

You could tell that the sun was starting up outside. The light inside the church strengthened. Light gathered itself up and streamed in. It fell through the coloured glass of the windows on to the columns, the floor. Bars of scarlet, green and blue. Little solid rainbows on the plaits and wreaths, on the statue of Our Lady of Blémont-la-Fontaine. Thérèse's statue. Fashioned according to Thérèse. Our Lady of would-be-saint Thérèse. Our Thérèse's Lady.

She stood ready to be taken around the village in procession after the harvest Mass. For this she had been brought out of her smart concrete chapel in the woods that the *curé* and the Bishop had built for her, for this she'd been set on top of the bier woven of corn. Wires twisted about her feet fastened her in place. When the bearers lifted her up she would not stagger or fall off.

She was child-sized. Plaster painted to look like polychromed wood. She was faintly gilded. Through the gold showed the greeny-blue streak of her dress, the yellow of her hair under her long veil. Cherubs and a cushiony cloud bore her up. Her hands were clasped and ecstatically raised, her bare feet rested on roses. Her eyes and sash were blue. She'd been redone since Thérèse saw her last. Her features were blurred under fresh paint and gilding, her fingers thickened. Her smile was unchangingly sweet.

She was the Virgin Mother of God. She was flat as a boy. She was the perfect mother who'd never had sex. To whom all earthly mothers had to aspire.

Easy to pretend your own mother never had sex. It meant you

didn't have to feel jealous when she went away to be with your father. It meant you could punish her by imagining you'd married your father yourself. You didn't need your mother, you told yourself. Anyway she wasn't there.

Antoinette had often prayed to the Mother of God. She'd aspired to her. But she hadn't been perfect. She'd had sex. She'd had a baby. She'd had red hair before it faded to gingery blonde. Her thick white skin had freckled and blotched in summer. She'd been broad-shouldered and tall. She'd often looked anxious. Her high voice called through the house. Listen! Where are you? Thérèse hadn't had time to get to know her.

Antoinette had gone away. Cancer had rubbed her out. Her voice got fainter. Her words stopped. She was off somewhere else where Thérèse couldn't follow her. Nothing left to live for, she'd mumbled right at the end. That's what death was. Just the next step. And the dying took it. Finally they desired it. They let go into it, stopped caring about anything, except death, they moved away and didn't miss you, they had their eyes fixed on death.

You won't die yet, Thérèse had whispered to her mother. And Antoinette's lips had twisted: oh yes I think I will.

She had gone off and abandoned Thérèse, she had expected her to grow up and manage on her own, in the end she'd forgotten her daughter, death was impatient and wouldn't wait.

Thérèse had been right behind her, forced to halt when Antoinette disappeared, left there alone on the brink, thrown back. Antoinette had pushed her away, hadn't let her come too, hadn't needed or wanted her company. She didn't care about how angry Thérèse felt, it didn't matter to her, she'd gone to a place where it wasn't important. Thérèse couldn't be angry with Antoinette: how could you be angry with someone who wasn't there, no mother to kiss the hurt better, take the pain away.

The pain was Thérèse's. It belonged to her. It stuck in her like stabbing swords. It lodged in her throat and made her choke. It burned, sour, in her stomach. It ticked in her blood, threatened to rip her apart and make her explode.

Thérèse had done the best she could. She'd found herself another mother, she'd been sold one ready-made by the priests of her Church. Perfect, that Mother of God, that pure Virgin, a holy doll who never felt angry or sexy and never went away. The convent was the only place where Thérèse could preserve that image intact.

Away from there it melted in the heat of her hands. It couldn't console her any more for Antoinette's loss. What she needed now was a funeral, a fire.

Around the bland-faced statue she piled the baskets of corn, the wreaths of wheat. All along the aisle, between the altar-rails and the door, she unrolled a narrow carpet, sprigs of barley and of oats.

After the harvest you set fire to the stubble and burned the fields. First ablaze then blackening. Scorched smell, red cinders flying in the wind, bald stalks. She took Léonie's lighter out of her pocket, flicked the silver top, pushed the leaping flame into the heap of harvest offerings.

Then, at last, after all these years, she saw her for the first time, that red and gold lady. The flames sliding up her forced her old clothes off, gave her new ones. With a red coat and slippers she flew. Skimmed into the air quick and bright as a rocket. She was outlined in gold, she held out her hands to her daughter, to pull her in, to teach her the steps of the dance.

Thérèse ran down the aisle of the church towards the door. After her ran the fire on red crackling feet. But Thérèse was too quick. Can't catch me. She flew with her one red wing. Her spine flared, one great red fin.

She jumped clear of those rags and tatters of flame. She cried *Maman*, and flung herself at the church door.

THE ALARM CLOCK

*L*éonie hadn't closed the shutters before getting into bed. She had pulled the heavy curtains of sprigged yellow chintz but had left a gap between them. As the darkness outside changed, and lightened, the space between the edges of the curtains became a streak of grey. A misty grey light leaked into the room, through Léonie's eyelashes that rubbed against her grey silk sleeve.

She focused on the chest of drawers next to the bed, the tin moon face of the alarm clock. It was an old one she liked because it had been Madeleine's. Green arrow hands, clear Roman numerals, stubby feet. It appeared to have stopped. No noisy tick. She stretched out an arm, picked it up, shook it. Was it really six o'clock? She wasn't sure.

Baptiste did not use alarm clocks. He liked to boast how he woke up exactly when he needed to, whatever the season. After his meeting last night, and his late session in the bar, he had slept deeply, snoring from time to time. But he was waking now. His head moved on the pillow, nearer to hers. Eyes firmly shut, he reached out and scooped her closer in, curved round her, both solid and soft. Still pretending to be fast asleep, he pulled the duvet almost over their heads to shut out the grey light.

Léonie whispered: I can't stop thinking about Thérèse. I've been dreaming about her all night.

Baptiste sighed and grunted.

Stupid girl.

Arms wrapped round her, he slid back into sleep. She lay inside his embrace, feet tangled up with his, mouth against his stubbly chin. He stroked her hip with one hand, muttered something.

She couldn't remember the dream exactly. About Thérèse. Something violent. The screech of bolts being drawn across, a red streamer tossed up into a vault of air.

Something was going to happen, to be upset. Léonie lay back, tried to reassert control over her world. She applied her usual formula for overcoming anxiety. She wandered in imagination through her house. She listed her numerous possessions one by one. She caressed her well-tended furniture. She chanted her triumphs of domestic organization, she recited her litany of solid objects, firm floors, walls that were not cracked and not defaced, foundations that did not crumble, a roof that was safe. She counted and inspected the contents of larders, china cabinets, cupboards. She raised her hand and set it all going. It clicked, whirred, chirruped. It was hers. It was her house. Her kingdom, firmly in her control. Peopled with daughters who looked like their mother and loved her comfortably and did as they were told.

No good. This morning the spell would not work.

Something glinted in the corner. Something started to shine. Léonie wriggled her chin over the edge of the duvet so that she could see. The room was emptying itself of darkness. The furniture was outlined with silvery light.

A light wind moved against the back of her neck. Not a draught but a wind. She'd shut the windows in here last night, she was certain. She lifted her head and looked.

The air seemed to ache and yawn. Like mayonnaise when it curdles, separates into tiny dots. The air was breaking up. Léonie fought against a memory which was coming too close. The shape of loss. The air hardening around what was lost for ever. Something might be disturbed, might break. She sucked in her breath.

She was inside what happened, and also outside. Her edges were of warm flesh, arms that held, contained. The world bent forwards, over her and into her, and she seized the world and leapt into it. Sweetness was her and it, her two hands grasping, her mouth demanding and receiving the lively flow. She was in a good place. Where the arms that held her would not let her drop, where her name was called over and over, where she was wanted, where she could stay and enjoy. The name of Léonie was the name of bliss. There was enough room for her. She did not have to go, to stop, to stand back. Rose sat easily, a baby on each arm. She looked from Léonie to Thérèse and she smiled. Of course I fed you both, silly. I had plenty of milk didn't I. Of course I fed you both. Rose, foster-mother, mother-in-law, second mother, fostering mother. Rose in her chair by the fire, feet up, blouse undone, a lapful of babies, a shout of joy, the smell of milk, there, my dears, there.

I took you both to the shrine in the woods, Rose said: what was left of it. It's what we always did with babies in the village. In the old days. I wanted you both to live, not to die like my child did. I dipped your feet in the spring. I popped you in, one after the other, just to make sure. That way you wouldn't come to any harm.

Rose leaned forward. She winked her green glass eye. Then she went away, quiet, abrupt, no goodbyes, nothing. Léonie jumped out of bed, to reach for her, call her back. She stood in the middle of the floor. She touched emptiness. Rose had gone.

THE WORDS

*L*éonie stood at the top of the kitchen stairs and faced the door of her old room. Her hand faltered out towards the china handle then slotted itself back into her woollen pocket. She fingered the roughly rolled edge of a seam, the cool cellophane wrapping her packet of cigarettes.

She wanted food inside her. Breakfast. To wall off the uncertain future. To shore her up. She wanted fresh white bread, salty and spongy under its crackling crust, spread with a slab of cold butter and a dollop of apricot jam scented with almonds. She wanted a cup of strong black coffee, well-sugared. More than this she wanted the best cigarette of the day: the first one. But she'd left her lighter in Thérèse's room last night and would have to go downstairs to find a match.

She was a coward who wanted to run away. The words she was frightened to say were fastened up inside this room. She thought she'd lost them, she'd forgotten she'd put them away in here. For twenty years. For thirty. Until Thérèse had arrived back and reminded her.

The grave in the cemetery had been forced open, made to give up its dead. At the same moment mouths had opened to shout words that Léonie had tried not to hear, tried to believe no one still spoke, would ever utter again. Death words shouted out in the night. Murderous red signs painted on the headstone of the grave. Léonie had to look steadily at what was rising up in her village, out of the grave of the war, the unburied and the undead arriving to lay hands upon them all, claim them for its own.

The murdered Jews had spent their last night in this room alongside the French peasant shot with them in the morning. They had chanted prayers in a language she could not understand. They had called out their own names and the name of the informer who had betrayed them. Léonie knew the names of the three members of the Jewish family, and she knew the name of the person who had led them to their deaths. She had heard them, night after night when she was ten years old. She had put the words away in here and left them because she was afraid.

She'd listed the contents of the room for her inventory simply as *bric à brac*. She'd kept the place as an extra store for junk overflowing from the attic. All the bits and pieces Madeleine had brought from the flat in suburban London she'd shared briefly with Maurice and then with Léonie. Maurice's books and army things, a clutter of valises and tin boxes and cracked leather bags. All the Englishness that Léonie had inherited from her father she had shut away in here. Then she had got on with marriage to a Frenchman, with becoming wholly French. She'd discouraged her daughters from ever entering this room. In case they heard those voices crying out and were frightened by them. In case they asked her to explain. But history was voices that came alive and shouted. Thérèse knew that, which was why she had come home.

Léonie had tried to cut Thérèse out of herself like the bad flesh from an apple. The rotten spot in her. Thérèse stood for the father, for God, for suffering. For everything that Léonie wanted to forget. But Thérèse had returned, she wouldn't be got rid of, she foretold a groan and heave of change.

Léonie would have to attend the enquiry into the desecrated grave, tell the lawyers the names of the slaughtered Jews buried there with Henri Taillé. She would have to confess that she had been silent all these years about the informer's identity. I had no real proof it was the priest, she'd argued with herself. So let them find it, she told herself now. Thérèse would have to accompany her, recount her side of the story. How much can either of us remember? Léonie thought: it's so long ago. Thérèse has begun writing it down. But I don't know that I'd want to rely on her memory alone. She'll have got half of it wrong.

She'd forgotten to put on her slippers. Her toes curled away from the cold floorboards. She took her hands out of her pockets and thrust them into her dressing-gown sleeves. Partly to warm herself. Partly to hold on to something, since she had no magic cigarette to stuff her mouth with, shut herself up with, defend herself with. Without a cigarette her sixth sense came back.

She had the idea that Thérèse was waiting for her on the other side of the door, along with the Jewish family and Henri Taillé. Her father Maurice was with them too. All she had to do was go in and join them, listen to what they had to say, unravel and reravel the different languages that they used.

She twisted the handle of the door. She opened it. She paused in the doorway, then went in.

The voices came from somewhere just ahead, the shadowy bit she couldn't see. She stepped forward, into the darkness, to find words.